GET THE AUDIOBOOK

I0685610

jljarvis.com/secrets

ALSO BY J.L. JARVIS

Drake & Wilde Mysteries
Love in the Time of Pumpkins
Secrets in the Hollow
Shadow of the Horseman

Standalones
A Kiss in the Rain
App-ily Ever After
Once Upon a Winter
The Red Rose
Highland Vow

Short Stories
Seasons of Love: A Short Story Collection
The Eleventh-Hour Pact
A Christmas Yarn
The Farmer and the Belle
Work-Crush Balance

Cedar Creek
Christmas at Cedar Creek
Snowstorm at Cedar Creek
Sunlight on Cedar Creek

Pine Harbor

Allison's Pine Harbor Summer
Evelyn's Pine Harbor Autumn
Lydia's Pine Harbor Christmas

Holiday House

The Christmas Cabin
The Winter Lodge
The Lighthouse
The Christmas Castle
The Beach House
The Christmas Tree Inn
The Holiday Hideaway

Highland Passage

Highland Passage
Knight Errant
Lost Bride

Highland Soldiers

The Enemy
The Betrayal
The Return
The Wanderer

American Hearts

Secret Hearts
Forbidden Hearts
Runaway Hearts

For more information, visit jljarvis.com.

Get monthly book news at news.jljarvis.com.

SECRETS IN THE HOLLOW

SECRETS IN THE HOLLOW

A DRAKE & WILDE MYSTERY
BOOK 2

J.L. JARVIS

SECRETS IN THE HOLLOW

Copyright © 2024 by J.L. Jarvis

All rights reserved.

No part of this book may be reproduced in any form or by any electronic or mechanical means, including information storage and retrieval systems, without written permission from the author, except for the use of brief quotations in a book review.

This is a work of fiction. Names, characters, places, and incidents are products of the author's imagination or are used fictitiously. Any resemblance to actual events, locales, or persons, living or dead, is entirely coincidental.

Published by Bookbinder Press

bookbinderpress.com

ISBN (ebook) 978-1-942767-66-4

ISBN (paperback) 978-1-942767-76-3

ONE

Iris Drake leaned against the cool windowpane, her breath fogging the glass. "Sfumato," she murmured, recalling a painting technique that meant 'to vanish like smoke.' In the faint glow of dawn, fog rolled over the Hudson River and clung to the land as if guarding its secrets. Soon, the sun would wash over the picturesque landscape. The sight should have been calming, but anxiety gripped her stomach with each passing moment.

She absently reached for the small Ph.D. charm on her keychain, a habit she hadn't shaken despite everything that had happened. The metal was cool against her skin, grounding her as memories of the past several days flooded back—the hidden messages in Washington Irving's works, the secret chamber beneath the Old Dutch Church, and the shadowy Wardens of Liberty. So much had changed since she'd arrived in Sleepy

Hollow, naïve to the secrets lurking beneath its quaint exterior.

A soft buzz from her phone broke the silence. A text from Jackson.

Meet me at the bridge. 20 minutes.

Iris's heart raced, not just from the urgency of the message, but from the thought of seeing him again. Their relationship had evolved from skeptical colleagues to something undefined but electric.

As she hurried down the stairs and pushed the door open, a rush of crisp morning air nipped at her cheeks. Fallen leaves crunched beneath her boots as she made her way down the sidewalk. The town was just beginning to stir, but an eerie stillness hung in the air as if Sleepy Hollow itself was holding its breath.

Iris rounded the corner and quickened her pace. The Headless Horseman bridge loomed ahead, shrouded in tendrils of mist rising from the river. And there, leaning against it, was Jackson with his tousled hair, leather jacket, and athletic frame that made her heart sing.

He straightened as she approached, his hazel eyes sweeping over her with a mixture of concern and warmth.

"Iris," he said, his voice rough from lack of sleep. "Thanks for coming."

"Of course," Iris replied, stepping closer.

She could smell his familiar scent—leather and coffee—and fought the urge to close the distance between them and bury her face in his chest.

Jackson ran a hand through his hair, a gesture she'd come to recognize as a sign of agitation.

"I couldn't sleep last night," he admitted. "I kept thinking about that map, the letters, and the... incident at the church."

Iris shivered, and not just from the cool air. The memory of their narrow escape from Dr. Grice's betrayal was still fresh.

"I know. I was restless all night."

Jackson's expression was grave.

"I think I've cracked another part of the cipher. The Wardens of Liberty are not just some innocuous flash-in-the-pan secret society. They're still active, and I think they're here in Sleepy Hollow."

With a shudder, she glanced around instinctively, suddenly aware of how exposed they were.

"Here?"

"Not here exactly, but close," Jackson amended, lowering his voice. He leaned in closer, and Iris's heart skipped a beat. "I found references to a meeting place somewhere in the woods north of town. We need to find it."

Iris bit her lip, excited at the prospect of a discovery but afraid of the danger that came with it. "Jackson, after what happened at the church... is it safe?"

His eyes met hers, intense and unwavering.

"Probably not," he admitted. "But we're in this too deep to back out now. Whatever the Wardens are protecting, they know we're looking for it. And the secrets they're keeping could change everything we know about history. If they're still active today, well, the possibilities are staggering."

As if to underscore his words, a sudden gust of wind swept over the bridge, carrying with it the faint sound of hoofbeats. Iris and Jackson both tensed, their eyes darting to the far end of the bridge, where mist swirled ominously.

"What was that?" Iris whispered, her hand instinctively finding Jackson's arm.

He nodded, his body coiled with tension. "It's just the wind playing tricks with our ears," he said, but his tone lacked conviction. After what they'd seen that night at the bridge—the impossible figure of the Headless Horseman charging through the mist—neither of them was quick to dismiss the strange occurrences in Sleepy Hollow.

As the sound faded, leaving only the gentle lapping of the river below, Jackson turned back to Iris. He covered her hand with his, then withdrew it in a gesture so tender it made her heart ache.

"I'm sorry I've put you in danger," he said softly. "I wish we could just walk away and pretend we never found any of it."

Iris leaned closer. "Could you really do that? Forget everything we've discovered?"

A wry smile tugged at Jackson's lips. "No," he admitted. "No more than you could."

Their eyes locked, and at that moment, Iris felt the full weight of their shared journey—the dangers they'd faced, the mysteries they'd unraveled, and the bond they'd formed. She could have kissed him right then, but his gaze broke away. When he looked back, he echoed a pact they'd made days before.

"So, still partners?"

Iris nodded, a smile breaking through despite the gravity of their situation. "Still partners," she affirmed.

As they left the bridge fading into the fog, Iris knew that whatever secrets Sleepy Hollow held, they would be there for each other, no matter how their world had been thrown off balance.

THE STREETS of Sleepy Hollow were still mostly empty as they walked to a small cafe on the corner. Neither of them spoke as they waited in line, recent events hanging between them.

Jackson handed her a cup of steaming coffee, and his fingers brushed hers. The small gesture sent a flicker of warmth through her, though it did little to settle her anxiety.

"I couldn't sleep last night either," Iris admitted as they settled at a small table near the window. "I kept mulling over the same things as you—the items we found and the... Horseman."

She barely whispered the last word, as if saying it out loud might somehow make it more real.

Jackson leaned back in his chair, studying her with those intense hazel eyes of his. He'd said little about the Horseman since that night—since they'd barely escaped whoever had been chasing them. Iris had hoped to find reassurance in his usual skepticism, but Jackson seemed as rattled as she was.

"It's a lot to take in," Jackson said quietly, finally breaking the silence. He took a long sip of his coffee, his gaze focused on the street outside. "There's so much going on here—and it's not just folklore."

Iris leaned in closer, her pulse quickening. "And it all seems to connect to the Wardens of Liberty."

"Absolutely," Jackson said, his voice firm. "There's a pattern in Washington's letters, and the more we decode, the more it points to something hidden here in Sleepy Hollow. I'm convinced it's not just some long-lost treasure or relic destined for a museum. It's... more dangerous."

The mention of danger made Iris's stomach sink. She had always known history could be powerful, but this was darker.

Before she could respond, Jackson reached into his jacket and pulled out a folded piece of parchment. He spread it across the table, revealing the rough sketch of a map they'd uncovered in the old Bible, its corners worn and faded with time.

"This," Jackson said, tapping the center of the map, "is our next step. There's something hidden at this location, something Washington didn't want to fall into the wrong hands."

Iris studied the map closely, her heart racing. "It looks like a burial site... near the Old Dutch Church."

Jackson nodded. "I've been combing through local

records. There's a legend about an underground chamber near that spot. Some say it was used during the Revolutionary War for secret meetings. Others believe it was a storehouse for Revolutionary War supplies, most likely munitions, or maybe gold."

Iris swallowed hard. "And you think that's where the Wardens hid... whatever it is we're looking for?"

"That's my theory," Jackson said, his eyes gleaming with excitement.

Iris couldn't believe it. "Buried treasure?"

Jackson lifted his shoulders. "Could be. Ordinarily, that would be my last guess, but we're not the only ones interested, so it does make me wonder. Whatever it is, Grice is still out there searching, too. I wouldn't be surprised if he's watching our every move. I can practically feel it."

The mention of Dr. Arthur Grice sent a chill through Iris. The man had always seemed... unsettling. Cold. Calculating. And after everything that had happened—after he'd threatened them with a gun—there was no telling how far he would go to protect whatever secrets the Wardens were hiding.

"So, what do we do now?" Iris asked, her voice steady despite the storm of emotions swirling inside her. "We can't just saunter over there with pickaxes and shovels slung over our shoulders."

"No." Jackson leaned forward, his gaze locking with hers. "We have to be careful. If Grice is involved with the Wardens, we can't let him know we're onto him. We move quietly, gather as much information as we can, and wait for an opportune moment."

Iris nodded, a sense of determination rising within her. This wasn't just historical research anymore. It had become all too real. If the Wardens of Liberty were intent on erasing the truth, she and Jackson had to find it first.

IRIS WAS ORGANIZING a new display of colonial-era artifacts when Margaret Verplanck, the director of the Heritage Center, appeared in the doorway. Margaret was an imposing figure despite her petite frame, with silver-streaked chestnut hair neatly pinned back and sharp green eyes that rarely missed a detail. Dressed in a tailored, moss-green jacket typical of her wardrobe that always seemed fitting for both academic meetings and the Center's events, Margaret carried herself with the confident authority of someone who had long served as the gatekeeper of Sleepy Hollow's rich heritage.

Today, however, her usually cheerful demeanor seemed slightly off, and a hint of concern creased her brow.

"Iris, do you have a moment?" Margaret asked, gesturing toward her office, her voice steady but lacking its usual warmth.

"Of course," Iris replied, setting down the delicate porcelain teacup she'd been arranging. She followed

Margaret, curiosity piqued by her boss's unusual mood.

As they walked, Iris was aware as ever of Margaret's imposing presence. The Verplanck name was as old as Sleepy Hollow itself, tied to the very foundations of the Hudson Valley. Margaret had always carried that legacy with grace, her knowledge of the area's history matched only by her dedication to preserving it. With her sharp mind and a deep sense of duty, Margaret was a mentor for Iris, a master of choosing and balancing research projects and garnering support from donors and the community. But today, that usual steadying influence seemed to be faltering.

Once inside the office, Margaret closed the door behind her and took a deep breath, the faint scent of her lavender hand cream wafting through the air. Her neatly organized desk was now cluttered with papers, a rare departure from her typically pristine workspace.

"I'm not quite sure how to say this," Margaret began, her voice soft but tinged with unease, "but Dr. Grice has... left us. Rather abruptly, I'm afraid."

Iris blinked in surprise. "Left? You mean he resigned?"

Margaret nodded, her lips pressed into a thin line. "He sent an email late last night. No explanation, no forwarding address. It's all very strange." Her fingers drummed lightly on the surface of her desk, a rare display of nerves. "To be honest, Iris, I'm relieved he's gone. There was always something... off about Arthur. He'd become increasingly secretive, almost paranoid. I caught him in the archives after hours more than once, rifling through documents he had no business accessing."

She leaned in, lowering her voice. "Just last week, we had a rather heated argument about some of the more... sensitive items in our collection. He was pushing for access to materials that have been restricted for decades. When I refused, well..." Margaret trailed off, a shadow crossing her face. "Let's just say his reaction was inappropriate. I was considering reporting him to the board before he suddenly resigned."

Iris frowned, processing this new information. "Do you think he took anything?"

Margaret sighed, worry lines creasing her forehead. "I'm not sure. We're still conducting an inventory. But if he did... well, some of those documents in the wrong hands could be dangerous. They're not just historical curiosities, Iris. They're keys to secrets some people would... go to great lengths to protect—or expose."

A mix of emotions flowed through Iris—relief, confusion, and, most of all, suspicion. Dr. Grice had always been an enigma, so his leaving actually didn't surprise her. Although he must have guessed she and Jackson would not have reported him to the police, given the secrecy of their research into the Wardens. So he wasn't in any danger of exposure to them. But they couldn't have all gone back to work as though nothing had happened. After all, the gun threat crossed over that line.

So good riddance, Dr. Grice.

"That is odd," Iris agreed, trying to keep her voice neutral. "What does this mean for the Center?"

Margaret's expression brightened, her shoulders relaxing a fraction. "Well, that's the other thing I wanted to discuss with you. Remember Professor Wilde, whom you assisted with some research?"

Iris's heart swelled at the mention of Jackson. "Yes, of course."

"Well, given how well you two worked together on that project, I've asked him to come on as a part-time consultant. He'll keep his position at Columbia, of course. We don't have that kind of budget. But he's agreed to work here a few hours a week on some of our more specialized projects."

As if on cue, a familiar figure appeared in the doorway.

"Speak of the devil," Margaret said with a smile.

Jackson Wilde leaned against the doorframe, a slight smirk playing at the corners of his mouth. "I hope I'm not interrupting," he said, his eyes meeting Iris's with a warmth that made her cheeks flush.

"Not at all," Margaret replied. "In fact, I was just about to tell Iris about your first project together."

Iris raised an eyebrow, intrigued. "Oh?"

Margaret reached into her desk drawer and pulled out a clear archival sleeve containing what looked like a weathered piece of parchment. "We've just acquired this fascinating document at an estate sale in the area. It appears to be related to Washington Irving, but we need to verify its authenticity and significance."

Jackson stepped fully into the office, his expression shifting from playful to intrigued. "What kind of document are we talking about?"

"It appears to be a letter, possibly written by Irving himself," Margaret explained. "But there are... inconsistencies that need to be examined. Given your previous work together on Irving-related matters, I thought you two would be perfect for this."

As Margaret handed the document to her, a jolt of excitement ran through Iris. This was precisely the kind of research she lived for.

"We'll get right on it," Iris said, her eyes meeting Jackson's. The spark between them was undeniable, a mixture of intellectual curiosity and a deeper connection she wasn't ready to define.

"Excellent," Margaret said, clearly pleased. "I'll leave you two to it, then. Let me know what you discover."

As they left Margaret's office, document in hand, Iris felt enthused and a little awestruck by the potential scope of their research. With Dr. Grice's sudden departure and Jackson's arrival, the quiet halls of the Heritage Center suddenly seemed full of possibility—and perhaps a hint of intrigue.

Jackson leaned in close as they walked, his voice low. "So, ready to uncover some more of Sleepy Hollow's secrets?"

Iris smiled, her pulse quickening. "Always."

TWO

I ris spread the weathered document carefully on the table in the Heritage Center's research room. Jackson leaned in close, his presence both comforting and distracting as they examined the faded ink.

"What do you think?" Iris asked, her eyes scanning the elegant script.

Jackson's brow furrowed. "It definitely looks like Irving's handwriting, but something feels... not quite right."

Iris nodded, reaching for her magnifying glass. As she examined the letter more closely, she noticed faint lines beneath some of the words. "Jackson, look at this. There are marks under certain letters."

He leaned in closer, his shoulder brushing hers. "Yeah. It's subtle, but it's there. Almost like..."

"A code," they said in unison, exchanging excited glances.

For the next few hours, they worked side by side, carefully documenting each marked letter and trying to decipher any pattern. As the sun began to set outside, Iris sat back with a sigh.

Something about the letter looked vaguely familiar. "This reminds me of the artifact we found during your last visit—the one with the strange engravings?"

Jackson's eyes lit up. "There might be a connection." He hurried to retrieve the artifact from its display case.

As they placed the two items side by side, the similarities became apparent. The markings on the artifact seemed to correspond with the subtle underlines in the letter.

"Iris," Jackson said, his voice low with excitement, "I think we've stumbled onto something big here."

Using the artifact as a key, they began to decode the hidden message in the letter. Slowly, words began to emerge: "Wardens... Liberty... Protect... Seal..." The message spoke of a secret society and mentioned the Old Dutch Church.

"Wardens of Liberty?" Iris repeated, a chill running down her spine.

Jackson shook his head, his expression a mix of excitement and concern. "We've come across that phrase before, but it was always dismissed as an obscure myth or a misinterpretation."

As they continued to decode, more of the message became clear. It spoke of a secret society dedicated to protecting some kind of powerful artifact or knowledge dating back to the founding of the nation.

"This is incredible," Iris breathed, her mind racing with the implications. "If this is real, it could rewrite parts of American history."

Jackson nodded, but his expression had grown serious. "It could also be dangerous. If there's any truth to this, there might be people who don't want it uncovered."

Iris couldn't believe what she was hearing. "So, you're saying we shouldn't look into it?"

"No!" His eyes sparkled. "That's just a disclaimer—to give you an out," Jackson said, his eyes gleaming with excitement.

"Oh, I'm in!" Iris said, too intrigued now to think about danger.

THE OLD DUTCH CHURCH, solid and stately, was a centuries-old testament to Sleepy Hollow's storied past. Evening had given way to twilight, casting shadows across the uneven ground. Gnarled branches reached out from ancient trees as if protecting crumbling tombstones that marked the final resting place of Sleepy Hollow's long-dead residents.

Jackson gave Iris a sideways glance, his brow furrowed. "You sure about this?"

Iris nodded, her gaze steady. "We can't stop now.

We're too close." She adjusted her scarf, but the uneasy feeling creeping up her spine wasn't caused by the cold.

At the side entrance of the church, a small wrought-iron gate stood between them and the historic cemetery. Jackson reached for the latch, and with a creak, the gate swung open. It was strangely quiet—too quiet for Sleepy Hollow, which was usually buzzing with tourists and locals enjoying the Halloween season.

"I don't like this," Jackson muttered under his breath as they made their way toward the side of the church where the oldest graves lay. The cool breeze had a sharp edge, so Iris pulled her jacket tighter around her while Jackson studied the map.

"This is the spot," Jackson said, his voice low as they stopped near an old, moss-covered gravestone. He held up the parchment map, its lines barely visible in the dimming light. "If Washington's letters are accurate, the chamber should be beneath this part of the cemetery."

Iris looked around, her heart beating faster. It was eerily quiet, with only the occasional rustle of leaves in the breeze breaking the stillness. With all the people who visited this place, it was hard to believe a secret chamber had been hiding buried for centuries.

"Are you sure?" she asked, her breath clouding the cold air. But she knew the answer. The journal had been clear. There was a hidden entrance to the chamber beneath the church, accessible only through a weathered stone near the base of one of the larger gravestones. Iris reached the spot first, kneeling in the damp grass to examine the area.

Jackson crouched beside her, squinting at the base of the gravestone. The moss-covered surface was etched with faint markings, almost completely worn away by time but just visible enough to make out a series of symbols.

"They match the ones in Washington's letters," Iris said, her heart quickening. "It's a cipher."

Jackson nodded, his expression serious. "These markings are telling us where to look. The entrance may be hidden, but it's got to be close."

As Jackson worked to decipher the symbols, Iris kept watch, her eyes darting to the shadows that crept through the cemetery. If something was lurking beyond the gravestones, waiting, she had to detect it.

After a few tense moments, Jackson sat up, brushing the dirt from his hands. "Got it. There's a hidden latch built into the stone, right... here."

He reached toward the base of the gravestone, feeling for the latch with his fingers. "I need something to dig with."

Iris checked her pockets and pulled out the contents—a crumpled receipt, a used tissue, and her keys.

Jackson took the keys and loosened some hardened dirt behind the gravestone. Iris held her breath. With a quiet *click*, the stone shifted, and they slid it aside to reveal a narrow opening in the ground.

"Oh my gosh!" Iris stared at the dark hole, her pulse racing.

Jackson grinned, his eyes gleaming with excitement. "Not exactly my words, but close enough."

Iris scanned the cemetery for any sign of movement, but they were alone.

Jackson pulled a penlight from his jacket pocket and aimed the beam into the opening. The narrow passage led down into the earth, its walls lined with old, uneven stones. A cold draft blew up from the depths, carrying with it the smell of damp earth and something else—something faintly metallic.

"Ready?" Jackson asked, offering her a hand.

Iris hesitated.

Jackson turned to her. "What? Don't tell me you're claustrophobic."

"No. Just arachnophobic."

"Spiders?"

She hoped that look was surprise, but it might have been condescension. With a nod, she said, "Spiders. Well, insects in general." Hearing Jackson take a quick breath, she quickly added, "I know spiders aren't insects, but I don't really care at the moment—"

"Iris," Jackson interrupted in a firm but calm voice. "It's okay. You don't have to do this."

"I'll be fine." Iris took a deep breath and grasped the hand Jackson offered. Its warmth and strength reassured her. Down the steep, narrow steps, slippery with moss and age, they descended.

Iris muttered, "And I might have a tiny bit of nyctophobia."

Jackson paused.

"The dark."

Afraid he'd send her back outside, Iris nudged him forward. "But it's okay. I'll be fine."

As they descended deeper into the ground, the walls seemed to close in around them, and the darkness pressed closer with every step. Finally reaching the bottom, Jackson stopped, pulled out a couple of headlamps, and gave one to Iris.

She wasn't sure whether to feel grateful or annoyed. "Thanks. This would have been really helpful a few cobwebs back." She put on the headlamp, turned it on, then shuddered as she pulled a sticky spiderweb from her hair and, unable to shake it loose, smeared it onto the stone wall.

The small stone chamber's walls were lined with shelves of artifacts—dusty old books, cracked pottery, and rusted tools. But it was the far side of the chamber that drew Iris's attention.

There, against the wall, stood a heavy stone door carved with intricate symbols—the same ones they had seen in Washington's letters.

"This is it," Jackson whispered, his voice filled with awe. "The hidden chamber."

Iris stepped closer to the door. Her heart pounded as she reached out to trace the symbols carved into the cold stone.

Jackson whispered. "Do you hear that?" He switched off his headlamp.

A faint sound echoed through the tunnel—footsteps —and they were getting closer.

"We're not alone," Iris whispered, her heart pounding.

Iris quickly doused her light as they pressed themselves against the damp wall. The footsteps grew louder, accompanied by hushed voices.

"... must be here somewhere," a gruff voice muttered.

"Keep looking," another replied. "We can't let them find it first."

Iris and Jackson hardly dared to breathe as the unknown searchers drew closer. The footsteps grew louder and closer. Iris's heart raced, and her breath came in shallow gasps. Whoever was in the passage with them wasn't trying to hide their presence.

Jackson's hand found hers in the dark, his grip firm.

The footsteps stopped just outside the chamber, and for a long, terrifying moment, there was only silence. Iris strained to hear, her mind racing. Were they about to be discovered? Was it Grice? Or someone worse?

The heavy grating of stone against stone filled the chamber.

"The door," Jackson whispered urgently. "They're sealing us in."

Panic flared in Iris's chest. "No!"

But by then, the stone door had shut. Jackson pulled her toward the opposite side of the chamber, where another door stood. His fingers fumbled in the dark, searching for a way to open it. Iris's heart pounded in her ears.

Frantically, she joined Jackson as, with headlamps switched on, they continued to search for a way to open the heavy stone door.

Just as the final scrape of the gravestone entrance above echoed through the tunnel outside, Jackson found the hidden latch. With a low groan, the heavy door slid open, revealing another passage beyond—this one wider and lined with old, rotting beams.

"Go!" Jackson urged, pushing Iris through the door before following her into the passage.

As Iris pushed herself up off her knees, her hand landed on a rolled piece of parchment. Assuming the opening door must have dislodged it, Iris scooped it up and stumbled forward as the chamber door rolled shut behind them. Iris's pulse raced as she and Jackson ran through the narrow passage. She didn't know where it led, only that they had to get as far away from the chamber—and whoever was behind them—as possible.

Iris didn't dare voice her growing fear that the way out might have collapsed or been sealed off decades ago. Her fears came to fruition when they arrived at the end of the tunnel.

They were feeling their way along every inch of the stone wall, hoping to find some way out.

Iris muttered, "I'd give anything for a pair of nitrile gloves. Did I say pair? I meant a box." Her light flickered and went out. "Oh, come on!"

In a steady voice, which Iris really loved at the moment, Jackson said, "We'll just have to dig our way out."

"Through the stone walls? With what—my keys—or what's left of them after grinding them down to dig our way in here?"

He said quietly, "Iris." Then he drew her against him and held her until she calmed down.

"I'm sorry." Iris brushed her hair from her face and assumed a composed demeanor she didn't feel. "It's just —you might be the Doctor Dolittle of spiders and dirt, but I'm not! And I just want a shower!"

He cupped her face in his hands. "I promise, if I can't get you a shower, I'll throw you into the Hudson myself."

Iris was stunned. "Please tell me you're kidding."

He chuckled and circled his arms around her. "Of course, I'm kidding." He glanced up. "Now, as much as I've loved this little chat, the walls might be stone, but the ceiling is dirt, so grab your keys, and let's dig."

While Iris scraped her keys through the dirt and spat out the clump that fell into her mouth, Jackson pulled something out of his pocket and joined her.

"What's that?" she asked, eyeing the tool in his hand.

"Bottle opener key ring."

"That sounds so good."

"What?"

"A bottle—of anything. To wash down the dirt."

At last, they unearthed a wooden hatch. It opened into a small clearing where the night sky loomed above them. Iris gasped for breath, her lungs burning from the exertion. Jackson hoisted her up and followed, closing the hatch behind him. Iris had never been so relieved to see stars twinkling faintly through a canopy of trees. Jackson grabbed her arm, pulling her onward. "We have to keep moving. If they know we're here, they'll be looking for us."

Iris nodded, adrenaline still coursing through her veins. If they were safe for the moment, she knew it wouldn't last.

THREE

As they hurried through the woods, the distant glow of the annual Great Jack-o'-Lantern Blaze came into view. The festival crowd would provide the perfect cover, but their enemies were closing in.

Thousands of intricately carved pumpkins appeared before them, all stacked and arranged to form shapes of creatures and structures in a riot of flickering orange light and grotesque shadows. Iris and Jackson melted into the crowd, their ragged breathing masked by the excited chatter of festivalgoers. Iris's heart hammered against her ribs, her historian's mind struggling to process the surreal shift from dusty archives to this festive Halloween carnival.

"Stay close," Jackson murmured, his hand touching the small of her back as they wound their way along the path leading through the displays. The warmth of his hand sent a shiver through her, despite their dire circumstances. "And keep your eyes open. They could be anywhere."

Iris nodded, trying to steady her breath. As they wove through elaborate pumpkin displays, her gaze darted from face to face, searching for their pursuers. A towering skeleton made of glowing pumpkins leered down at them, its hollow eyes seeming to follow their movements.

"This is insane," Iris whispered, leaning closer to Jackson. "How did we go from decoding Revolutionary War letters to running for our lives?"

Jackson's jaw tightened, his eyes scanning the crowd. "Welcome to the ugly side of history, Dr. Drake. Some secrets don't want to be found."

As they passed a pumpkin arch, Iris caught a glimpse of a familiar face in the crowd. Her blood ran cold.

"Jackson," she hissed, gripping his arm. "Three o'clock. Grice."

Jackson's head snapped around, his body tensing. Dr. Grice, a former colleague turned adversary, was pushing through the crowd, his hawkish gaze sweeping the area.

"Move," Jackson ordered, guiding Iris toward a denser part of the crowd. They ducked behind a massive pumpkin dinosaur, its towering body shrouding the ground in its shadow.

"What now?" Iris asked, her mind racing. "We can't keep running forever."

Jackson's eyes met hers with determination and a softness flickering in their depths.

"We don't. We find answers." He pulled out his phone, thumbs flying over the screen. "I've got a contact at the National Archives. If anyone can shed light on the Wardens of Liberty, it's her."

Iris raised an eyebrow. "The National Archives in Washington? There's a lot about you I don't know."

A ghost of a smile touched Jackson's lips. "Let's hope it stays that way. Keeps things intriguing."

Before Iris could respond, a child's scream pierced the air. They whirled around to see a young boy pointing at something behind them. Iris's heart stopped as she followed his gaze.

There, emerging from the shadows cast by the pumpkin dragon, was a figure straight out of Washington Irving's nightmares. Tall, broad-shouldered, and headless, it advanced toward them with purposeful strides.

"Run!" Jackson shouted, grabbing Iris's hand.

They sprinted through the festival, dodging confused onlookers and toppling smaller pumpkin displays. Iris's lungs burned, and her legs protested as they fled. Behind them, she could hear the heavy footfalls of their pursuer, unnaturally fast.

As they made a run for the trees, Iris's heart pounded along with the beat of each footstep. Taking cover behind a large oak, they watched and waited. As the figure approached, Jackson lunged and tackled the man to the ground. Iris rushed over and put her full weight into pinning him down by the ankles.

"Who are you? What are you after?" Jackson demanded as he gripped the man's shoulders and pulled off his mask.

Their captive was younger than Iris expected, fear etched into his pale features. "I can't—they'll kill me if I talk," he stammered.

"Who? The Wardens?" Iris pressed, crouching down. "Is that who you're working for?"

The man's eyes widened at the name, confirming Iris's suspicion. But before they could press further, he jerked his feet loose, kicked Iris in the stomach, then kneed Jackson's jaw, throwing him off balance. In a flash, their assailant was gone, swallowed by the shadows.

"Damn it!" Jackson cursed, rubbing his jaw.

Iris pulled herself up, her mind reeling.

"So, the Wardens are real."

Jackson nodded grimly. "And terrified of what we might uncover."

As he helped Iris up, she asked, "Now what?"

Jackson said, "The Heritage Center. We need to revisit the archives."

Iris nodded, and they headed for the darkened streets of Sleepy Hollow.

As THEY MADE their way out of the woods, Iris jumped at every shadow, her nerves frayed.

"My place is around the corner," she whispered. "We need to regroup."

At least I do. I need to recover.

"No. If they know who we are, then they'll know—or find out—where you live."

The thought of their mysterious pursuer stalking her home sent a shiver of terror through Iris. She picked up her pace, walking closer to Jackson. "So, someone—or any number of people could be lurking outside my apartment."

Jackson nodded, his jaw clenched. "They're not amateurs. Whoever these people are, they're not afraid to get physical."

Iris rounded a corner and slipped into a narrow alleyway, momentarily hidden from view. She leaned against a brick wall while she caught her breath. Heart racing, nerves frayed, she closed her eyes and willed herself to calm down.

Jackson stood beside her. "Hey." His voice was low and steady, pulling her back to the present. "You okay?"

Iris nodded, though her heart still thudded uncomfortably. "Yeah... Actually, no. But I will be."

"Come here." Jackson drew her into his arms and held her.

When she'd calmed down, she opened her eyes and looked up at him, finding comfort in his steady gaze. He was so sure it somehow anchored her. She managed a small, grateful smile. "I didn't expect it to get this dangerous."

Jackson's lips quirked into a faint smile. "Neither did I, but hey, we signed up for this adventure, right?"

A wry chuckle escaped her. "I don't remember signing up for near-death experiences."

"Gotta read the fine print," he teased, his smile widening.

The tension eased between them, just for a moment, and for that, Iris was grateful.

THE HERITAGE CENTER LOOMED AHEAD, a brooding silhouette against the night sky. There, they hoped to comb through the archives for answers. As they approached, Jackson fished out a set of lock picks.

"Seriously?" Iris asked, keeping watch as he worked on the door. "Where does a history professor learn to pick locks?"

"Summer job," Jackson grunted, focused on the lock.

"Doing what? Cracking safes?"

"Locksmith—well, his assistant." The lock clicked open, and they slipped inside. Iris quickly disarmed the security system. The familiar scent of old books and polished wood enveloped them as they made their way to the archives.

"There's a connection in here somewhere," Jackson

said, rifling through folders. "Something that links the Wardens to whatever's in that chamber."

Iris nodded, her mind already cataloging possibilities. She booted up a computer, fingers flying over the keys as she accessed digitized records. "There's got to be a pattern, something we missed..."

As they worked, the air grew thick with tension. Every creak of the old building sent Iris's heart racing.

Jackson muttered, "I could use a good research assistant right now."

"Couldn't we all?" Iris said as she scanned the text on her screen.

"No, I mean, I've got one at school. He's a genius with a computer, but he really kicks ass at speed reading old handwritten documents." Jackson pulled out his phone and searched through his contacts. "Danforth, Denton... There he is, Arjun Desai." Jackson stopped. With a shake of his head, he put his phone back in his pocket. "Except I can't drag Arjun up here and put one more person in danger." With a sigh, Jackson returned to his research.

"Wait," Jackson said suddenly, his voice tight with excitement. "Look at this."

Iris hurried over, peering at the document in his hands. It was a letter, dated 1783, from a prominent Sleepy Hollow resident to George Washington. Her eyes widened as she read.

"'The artifact is secure,'" she whispered, tracing the words. "'Its power remains hidden, as do the truths it could reveal. The Wardens stand ready to protect it, now, tomorrow, and always.'"

Jackson's gaze met Iris's, and a spark of shared understanding passed between them.

"This isn't just about Revolutionary War secrets," he said. "Whatever's in that chamber, it's... more."

Before Iris could respond, a loud crash echoed through the building. They froze, eyes locked in the dim light.

Heavy footsteps approached, slow and deliberate. Iris's breath caught in her throat as a shadow fell across the frosted glass of the archive room door. Her pulse pounded in her ears. Beside her, Jackson rested his hand on her arm as they listened and waited. The door creaked as though someone was testing it—pushing gently to see if it was locked.

Then, after a moment that felt like an eternity, the footsteps retreated.

Jackson let out a slow breath, his grip on Iris's arm loosening.

"We need to move," Iris whispered.

Jackson opened a window and held Iris's wrists while she safely dropped a few feet to the ground, and then he followed. He hesitated, searching for signs of their pursuer, but it was still. Together, they disappeared into the darkness, leaving the Heritage Center behind. But the danger was out there somewhere.

IN THE STILLNESS of early morning, Iris sat at the small kitchen table in her apartment, staring at the ancient wooden box that had caused them so much trouble. They'd argued over whether they ought to return to retrieve it, but they needed to examine its contents, so the decision was made. Sunlight filtering through the curtains made the old wood gleam, its intricate carvings seeming to hold even more secrets under the warmth of the daylight.

Jackson stood by the window, arms crossed over his chest, his brow furrowed in thought as he stared out at the quiet streets below. The tension between them hadn't eased since the night before, although it had shifted. There was a lingering frustration over how close they'd come to getting answers, only to watch them slip away.

"We can't just keep running," Iris said, breaking the tense silence.

Jackson turned, his hazel eyes dark with worry. "No, but we can't ignore the fact that the Wardens are watching our every move, either."

Iris nodded, her gaze drifting to the leather-bound journal they'd discovered. She reached for it, her fingers trembling slightly. As she opened the book, Jackson moved to sit beside her. His warmth comforted her.

The faded ink seemed to pulse with secrets as Iris read aloud.

"'October 12, 1799,'" she began, her voice barely above a whisper. "'The time grows short. We've secured the artifact in the chamber beneath the Dutch

Church,'" Iris and Jackson exchanged knowing looks.
"'But I fear it will not remain hidden for long. The veil
between worlds weakens, and the signs of the Horseman's return are upon us.'"

Jackson leaned in closer, his breath warm on her
cheek. "The Horseman again. It always comes back to
him."

Iris nodded, a chill running down her spine. She
turned the page, her heart quickening as she read the
next entry.

"'October 15, 1799. It has begun. The Horseman
rides again. The chamber must remain sealed, but I fear
it is only a matter of time before the artifact falls into
the wrong hands.'"

Iris whispered, "'The chamber beneath the Dutch
Church.' We had the wrong chamber."

Jackson's eyes narrowed. "How many chambers are
there?"

"Maybe   it's   an   underground   system—all
connected."

Jackson furrowed his eyebrows. "Maybe. It would
have been a great way to move things—munitions,
gold..."

Iris interrupted. "Or historical artifacts like the one
in that letter."

Jackson nodded slowly. "And, if your theory holds,
and tunnels connect the chambers, then the artifact
could have been moved—"

"By the Wardens."

Silence fell between them, heavy with the burden

of centuries-old secrets. As they bent their heads over the journal, a shadow passed by the window. Iris's head snapped up, her heart racing. "Did you see that?"

Jackson was already moving, peering out onto the quiet street below. "Nothing," he said, but his tense posture betrayed his unease.

Iris joined him at the window, the hair on the back of her neck standing on end. "They're out there, aren't they? Watching us."

Jackson nodded grimly. "Pack some things. It's not safe to stay here."

While Iris threw a few clothes in a bag, Jackson packed up the box and his research papers into his leather satchel.

They couldn't go straight to the graveyard chamber in broad daylight, but they might be able to slip inside the Old Dutch Church unobserved.

Iris slung a backpack over her shoulder and joined Jackson at the door.

He paused and turned to face her. "Are you sure about this? It's not too late. You could still walk away."

For a second, Iris was tempted. She thought of her quiet life before all this, the safety of academic theories and dusty archives. But the way her pulse quickened when she and Jackson were on the verge of a break-through was too much to resist.

"No," she said firmly. "I'm in."

A slow smile spread across Jackson's face, tinged with admiration. "Then let's go."

As they stepped out into the crisp morning air, Iris

felt a mix of fear and exhilaration. Whatever lay beneath the Old Dutch Church, whatever secrets the Wardens were protecting, were out there. But so was the danger. There was always a chance they might walk into a trap, but the pull of the mystery was too strong to resist.

FOUR

Ten minutes from Sleepy Hollow, Jackson turned his Land Rover onto a private gravel drive that led to a small riverfront cottage on a wooded plot of land. There wasn't another building in sight.

Iris blinked. "Um, Jackson? This is... nice. But... waterfront acreage in Westchester? You never mentioned you were rich."

He didn't seem surprised by the question. "It didn't come up in conversation." He made a halfhearted attempt to shrug it off. "It's a family retreat—handed down over generations."

Shaking her head, she said, "Well, your ancestors would love the current real estate market!" She stopped herself from guessing how many millions the land alone must be worth. Inside, she found a surprisingly cozy space with wide plank wood flooring and overhead beams, a small upscale kitchen in the corner, and a bedroom off to one side.

Jackson dropped his satchel on an old oak kitchen table serving as a desk, judging by the haphazard piles of books and papers on it. He turned on the gas fireplace, then grabbed Iris's bag. "You're in here."

She followed him into a small bedroom decorated in earth tones, with its own fireplace, a tall utilitarian dresser, and a bed that took up most of the space. She wasn't sure what to say. Unless there was a secret door off the great room, this was his bedroom. Where was he going to sleep? Not that she hadn't thought about being with him. But they weren't there yet. Realizing she hadn't moved, she now feared her face had revealed too much.

Jackson gestured toward the great room. "I'll take the couch."

That confirmed it. He'd guessed her thoughts, and now things were awkward. "No, Jackson. You won't. I sleep better on couches." *Liar.* "So that's the end of it."

He looked doubtful, but Iris took her overnight bag out of the bedroom and set it down beside the sofa. With that settled, her thoughts returned to Sleepy Hollow. Mostly.

The warm glow of the fireplace did little to ease the tension. Shadows danced on the walls, cast by the flickering flames, creating an atmosphere of mystery that matched their current predicament. Iris sat at the small wooden table, her fingers tracing the edges of the cryptic document they'd recovered during their escape from the underground chamber. The paper felt rough beneath her fingertips, a tangible link to the past they were trying to unravel.

Jackson paced the room, his footsteps muffled by the worn rug. His brow was furrowed in concentration, and Iris couldn't help but admire the intensity of his focus. The events of the past few days had brought them closer, and she found herself increasingly aware of his presence.

"It has to be connected to the chambers we found it in," Iris said, her voice barely above a whisper. The quiet of the cottage seemed to demand discretion, as if the very walls might be listening. "But it wasn't on the shelves with the other books and artifacts. It was wedged into the door. I only found it because it fell when we opened the door."

Jackson nodded, running a hand through his hair. "Agreed. Someone must have hidden it in a hurry. But why?"

Without an answer, Iris spread the document on the table, carefully smoothing its creased surface. The paper was old, its edges frayed and yellowed with age, but the ink remained remarkably clear—a series of numbers and symbols that made no immediate sense. The lamplight caught the edges of the paper, high-lighting its imperfections and adding to its air of mystery.

"It's definitely a cipher," she murmured, leaning closer to examine the markings. Her eyes strained in the soft light, picking out patterns and repetitions. "Similar

to the ones we've seen in Washington's letters, but...
different somehow."

Jackson pulled up a chair to join her. His presence
at her side warmed Iris.

"The style is familiar," he said, pointing to a recur-
ring symbol. His finger brushed against Iris's, sending a
frisson of energy through her. "Look at how this mark is
used—it's almost like a key."

For the next few hours, they worked in tandem,
scribbling notes and testing different decoding methods.
The room grew quiet except for the scratching of
pencils and the occasional frustrated sigh. Scattered
slips of paper multiplied on the table as the night wore
on, a testament to their determination.

Iris leaned back, rubbing her eyes. The symbols on
the page seemed to dance before her, mocking their
efforts. "This is impossible," she groaned, pushing back
from the table. The chair scraped against the wooden
floor, sounding harsh in the quiet room. "We're missing
something."

Jackson stretched, his joints popping audibly. He
looked as tired as Iris felt, dark circles forming under his
eyes. "Maybe we need a break. Fresh eyes might help."

Iris nodded, realizing how stiff she'd become. As she
stood, her stomach growled loudly, prompting a chuckle
from Jackson. The sound broke the tension, reminding
them both that they were still human, still vulnerable to
mundane needs despite the extraordinary circumstances they found themselves in.

"I think that's our cue for dinner," he said with a

smile that didn't quite reach his eyes. "I'll see what I can throw together."

In the small kitchen, Jackson moved with practiced ease, reheating a simple meal of soup and bread. The domestic scene felt oddly normal, a stark contrast to the mystery that consumed their days. As they ate, the conversation drifted from the cipher to their shared love of history.

"What made you choose this field?" Jackson asked, tearing off a piece of bread. "Why history?"

Iris pondered the question, stirring her soup absently. "I've always been fascinated by the stories behind events," she said finally. "The human element that textbooks often gloss over. What about you?"

A shadow passed over Jackson's face, there and gone so quickly Iris almost thought she'd imagined it. "Family tradition, I suppose," he said, his tone neutral. "The Wildes have always been... involved in historical research."

There was something in his voice, a weight to his words, that piqued Iris's curiosity. "Jackson," she said softly, reaching across the table to touch his hand. "What aren't you telling me?"

He paused, his spoon halfway to his mouth. For a moment, Iris thought he might deflect, but then he sighed, setting down his utensil. The weight of unspoken secrets seemed to settle on his shoulders.

"About my family," he began, his voice low and hesitant. "There's something I haven't told you—or anyone else. But since I've dragged you into this..."

Iris leaned forward, her food forgotten. The air in the room seemed to thicken with anticipation.

Jackson took a deep breath, his eyes meeting hers with an intensity that made her breath catch. "I'm from here—as were my ancestors. My great-great-grandfather wasn't just a resident of Sleepy Hollow. He was part of a secret society."

"Not—"

"The Wardens of Liberty."

The name sent a chill down Iris's spine, goosebumps rising on her arms despite the warmth of the room. "So, your interest didn't just stem from random research."

He shook his head. "And if the Wardens are at the heart of all this, then my family's involved—for good or for bad," Jackson admitted, his voice barely above a whisper. "The underground chambers, the ciphers—it all seems to lead back to them, and I want to know how."

Iris's mind raced with questions, each one spawning a dozen more. "The cipher—"

"I'm not a genius code breaker. I mean, I'm good, but I found the original cipher in some old family papers. The others kind of spun out from there."

The implications of Jackson's revelation were staggering. Before she could voice any more questions, Jackson stood abruptly.

"Which reminds me, we should get back to the cipher," he said, his tone making it clear the conversation was over—for now. The abrupt shift left Iris reeling, but she recognized the need to focus on the task at hand.

Returning to their work with renewed focus, they pored over the document once more. It wasn't until well past midnight that Iris felt a spark of recognition.

"Jackson," she breathed, excitement building in her voice. "I think I've got it. Look at this."

She pointed to a section of the text, and Jackson leaned in close, his shoulder brushing hers. The closeness sent a jolt through Iris, but she forced herself to focus on the breakthrough.

Jackson read aloud, his voice filled with a mixture of awe and trepidation. "'Beneath the hollow, secrets dwell, the covenant's tale, brave hearts will tell.'"

"The covenant?" Iris frowned, her mind already racing with possibilities. "What the heck does that mean?"

Jackson's expression grew serious, the lamplight casting deep shadows across his face. "I'm not sure, but it dovetails with everything I know about my family and the Wardens."

Over the next hour, Jackson revealed more about his family's history with the secret society. The Wardens of Liberty, he explained, had roots going back to the Revolutionary War. They were dedicated to protecting certain secrets—secrets that could change the course of history if revealed.

"Come on, Jackson. You can't just drop a bombshell like that and not explain it."

"I don't know. I'm not a warden, so I was never let in on the secrets."

"But why keep the group hidden for so long?" Iris asked, struggling to comprehend the scale of the conspiracy. "Wouldn't it have outlived its purpose?"

"That's what we need to find out," Jackson replied, determination hardening his voice. "And I think the answer lies in those underground chambers."

Iris inwardly groaned. *More spiders. Yay.*

With the cipher partially decoded and this new information weighing heavily on their minds, they decided to explore the tunnel entrance they'd discovered earlier. Grabbing flashlights and jackets, they set out into the cool night air.

The moon hung low in the sky, partially obscured by gauzy clouds. Iris's breath fogged in the chilly air as she and Jackson made their way through the silent streets of Sleepy Hollow. The town seemed different at night, its quaint charm replaced by an air of mystery and hidden peril.

Behind a cluster of rocks near the old church, the entrance to the tunnel system lay hidden. As they approached, Iris shivered. *I can do this. I am not going to panic.*

Jackson moved a concealing bush aside to reveal the wooden hatch. "Ladies first," he said with a wry smile, gesturing for Iris to enter.

"Thanks," she said, hoping he hadn't seen her grimace.

Taking a deep breath, Iris clicked on her headlamp

and climbed down into the tunnel. The air inside was thick with the scent of damp earth. As they descended, the temperature dropped, and the sounds of the outside world faded away.

They retraced their steps back to the chamber door but couldn't find the latch. After running his hand along the entire door, Iris stared for a moment.

"The paper!"

Jackson stared blankly at her.

"You're the locksmith."

"Assistant. It was just a summer job."

"Whatever. If you want to keep a lock from latching..."

Jackson's face lit up. "The paper!"

Iris couldn't help feeling pleased with herself. As she pulled a credit card from her bra, Jackson raised an eyebrow.

"What? It's convenient and pickpocket-proof."

His mouth twitched at the corner as he retrieved his own credit card from his more traditional wallet, and he joined Iris, sliding a card along the gap between the stone door and doorframe. With a click, they were in.

Her headlamp revealed the now familiar rough-hewn walls and support beams, but the shelves were what interested them.

They'd been thumbing through crumbling books for a couple of minutes when Iris paused, wincing. "If we could just take one book with us..."

Jackson shook his head slowly.

Before he had a chance to speak, she added, "I know. The oxygen and pollution would deteriorate it."

Jackson stared at the books. "Actually, Revolutionary War era paper was made of cotton and linen, so it would fare better than newer paper made from wood, but—" He winced. "No, we can't risk it."

The sound of approaching footsteps sent a jolt of adrenaline through Iris, her heart suddenly pounding in her chest.

"Lights off," Jackson hissed, grabbing Iris's arm, and pulling her into a small alcove. They pressed against the wall, barely daring to breathe as the footsteps grew louder.

A beam of light swept past their hiding spot, and Iris caught a glimpse. *Dr. Grice!* His face was set in a grim expression, his eyes scanning the tunnel as if searching for something—or someone.

Once the footsteps faded and Grice's light disappeared around a bend, Jackson and Iris headed for the exit. Fleeing back to the entrance, they emerged into the night. The cool air was a welcome shock after the stuffy confines of the tunnel.

"That was too close," Iris said, her voice shaky. The near encounter had left her rattled.

Jackson nodded grimly, his eyes scanning the area for any sign of pursuit. "But now we know for sure— there's something down there that Grice and the Wardens don't want us to find."

"It's almost as if someone's standing guard over the

tunnels—like a night watchman." Her breath caught in her throat. "Or a warden."

As they walked back to the cottage, a sense of anticipation intensified between them. They were on the verge of uncovering something. But with Grice and the Wardens closing in, it was a race against the unknown. Whatever secrets lay hidden in the tunnels below had to be uncovered before it was too late.

As they reached the cottage, Iris paused, looking back at the sleeping town. In the distance, the old church stood silhouetted against the night sky, a silent guardian of centuries-old secrets. But tonight, they'd stepped deeper into the mystery, and that brought them closer to danger.

Jackson's hand on her shoulder brought her back to the present. "We should get some rest," he said softly. "Tomorrow, we dive deeper."

Iris nodded and followed him inside. As she made up the sofa, her mind raced with the events of the night. The cipher, the Wardens, the tunnels—it all swirled together. And they were more deeply embroiled.

FIVE

The morning sun filtered through the cottage windows, casting long shadows across the worn wooden floor. Iris sat at the kitchen table, nursing a cup of coffee, her mind still reeling from the previous night's revelations. The aroma of freshly brewed coffee mingled with the musty scent of old books and papers scattered across the table, creating an atmosphere thick with mystery.

Jackson stood by the window, his posture tense as he gazed out at the mist obscuring the landscape of Sleepy Hollow. A cold snap had blanketed the river and its banks with dense fog. It clung to the trees, shrouding the town in an ethereal haze that seemed fitting, given the secrets they were trying to uncover. Iris watched him, noting the way his shoulders drooped as if carrying an invisible weight.

"We need to know more," Iris said, breaking the silence. Her voice sounded loud in the quiet room despite her soft tone. "About your family, about the Wardens. Everything."

Jackson turned to face her, his expression a combination of determination and apprehension. The morning light cast half his face in shadow, giving him an almost mythical appearance.

"You're right," he said after a moment's hesitation. "It's time I showed you something."

He disappeared into his bedroom, leaving Iris alone with her thoughts. She took another sip of coffee, savoring its warmth and the jolt of caffeine. The past few days had left her feeling off balance, as if she'd stepped into one of the very histories she'd spent her life studying.

Jackson returned moments later with an old, leather-bound box. The box itself was a work of art, its surface adorned with intricate designs that spoke of a craftsman's careful touch. As he set it on the table, the musty scent of aged paper and ink wafted from within.

"This belonged to my great-great-grandfather," Jackson explained, his fingers tracing the intricate designs on the box's surface. There was a reverence in his touch, a connection to the past that Iris found both fascinating and slightly unnerving. "I've never shown it to anyone before."

Jackson reached into the box, his fingers brushing past yellowed letters and faded documents. He pulled out a sepia-toned photograph, holding it up to the lamplight.

"This is Alexander Wilde," he said, his voice tinged

with pride and apprehension. The photograph showed a stern-looking man with a thick beard, dressed in the formal attire of the late 19th century. His eyes seemed to pierce through time, challenging the viewer. "He was my great-great-grandfather and one of the most influential members of the Wardens of Liberty during his time."

Iris leaned closer, studying the image. "He looks... formidable," she said, choosing her words carefully.

Jackson nodded, a wry smile tugging at his lips. "That's one way to put it. From what I've pieced together, he was brilliant but also deeply committed to the Wardens' cause. He believed there were forces at work trying to undermine the very foundations of America."

"But you said the Wardens go back further than this," Iris prompted, her historian's curiosity piqued.

"Much further," Jackson confirmed. He set the photograph aside and carefully extracted an older, more fragile document from the box. The paper was brittle, its edges frayed, but the ink remained remarkably clear. "This letter dates back to 1789, just after the Constitution was ratified. It's from one of the original founders of the Wardens of Liberty."

Iris's eyes widened as she realized the historical significance of what she was seeing. "May I?" she asked, holding out her hand.

Jackson hesitated for a moment before carefully passing her the letter. "My family has been part of the Wardens for generations," he explained as Iris began to read. "Each generation plays their role in protecting the secrets and ideals the organization was founded to preserve."

Iris scanned the letter, her breath catching as she read:

"My dear friend, the burden we bear grows heavier with each passing day. The knowledge we protect could tear this fragile union apart if it were to be revealed. We must redouble our efforts to safeguard the covenant. The future of our nation depends on it."

She looked up at Jackson, her mind reeling from the implications. "This is incredible, Jackson. Your family has been at the center of this for over two centuries?"

Jackson nodded, his expression somber. "It's a legacy that's been passed down, along with the responsibility it carries. Alexander, my great-great-grandfather, took that duty perhaps more seriously than any before him. He expanded the Wardens' influence, developed new codes and ciphers, and went to great lengths to ensure the secrets remained hidden."

He pulled out another document, this one a journal entry in Alexander's hand. "He writes about 'securing the future of liberty' and 'protecting the true spirit of the Revolution.' But he was also paranoid, convinced that there were always enemies trying to uncover what the Wardens had hidden."

Iris absorbed this information, her historian's mind already connecting dots and forming theories. "So, the Wardens of Liberty aren't just some historical footnote. They're an ongoing organization with roots stretching back to the founding of our nation—sworn to protect... something. But what?" She murmured, "'We hold these truths to be self-evident, that all men are created equal, that they are endowed by their Creator with certain unalienable Rights...'"

Jackson leaned in, intrigued. 'You think the Seal might be connected to protecting these rights?'

"It's just a theory," Iris replied, "but yes."

Jackson nodded. "And somehow, we've stumbled onto something they've been protecting for generations. Whatever it is, whatever secrets lie hidden in those tunnels, they're part of something much bigger than we initially thought."

The implications of this revelation settled over them both. Iris looked at Jackson, seeing him in a new light. He wasn't just a fellow historian anymore; he was a living link to a secret history that had shaped their nation from the shadows.

"Jackson," she said softly, "why are you telling me all this?"

He met her gaze, his eyes filled with determination and uncertainty. "Because I trust you. And because I think we're onto something that might need to come to light despite centuries of secrecy."

The room fell silent as his words sank in. What secrets might they unearth?

Jackson cleared his throat, breaking the spell. "We need to go to the library," he said, standing up. "There are town records, old newspapers—things that might corroborate what we're seeing here."

THE SLEEPY HOLLOW PUBLIC LIBRARY was a grand old building with an imposing stone facade harkening back to another era. Inside, the librarian, an elderly woman with sharp eyes behind thick glasses, regarded them suspiciously as they requested access to the archives.

"Historical research," Jackson explained smoothly. "We're working on a paper about Sleepy Hollow's role in the post-Revolutionary War period."

The librarian's expression softened slightly. "Well, it's good to see young people taking an interest in history. The archive room is downstairs. Leave everything as you found it."

In the archive room, surrounded by shelves laden with dusty tomes and boxes of fragile documents, Iris and Jackson dove into their research. They cross-referenced dates and names from Alexander's journal with historical events, building a timeline that spanned centuries.

What they found was staggering. There were subtle influences on local politics, unexplained disappearances of certain documents, and a pattern of the Wilde family's presence at crucial moments in the town's history. It was as if the Wardens had been quietly shaping events from the shadows, their influence felt but never seen.

"Look at this," Iris said, pointing to an old newspaper article. "In 1872, there was a fire at the town hall. A lot of records were destroyed."

Jackson leaned over her shoulder, his breath warm on her cheek. "And according to this ledger, my great-great-grandfather made a substantial donation to rebuild the hall just a week later."

"It's like they were puppet masters," Iris whispered, her eyes wide as she connected yet another dot in their growing web of conspiracy. "But to what end? What were they protecting that was so important?"

As the day wore on, they found themselves no closer to understanding the true nature of the covenant. But one thing was becoming increasingly clear—the Wardens of Liberty were far more influential and far-reaching than they had initially believed.

They worked through lunch, too engrossed in their discoveries to notice the passage of time. It was only when the librarian came to inform them that the library would be closing soon that they realized how late it had grown.

Gathering their notes and returning the documents to their proper places, Iris and Jackson left the library. The sun was setting, shining its last rays of light on all but the dark secrets they'd spent the day uncovering.

"We need to go back into those tunnels," Jackson said as they approached the cottage.

Iris winced at the mention of the tunnels. "Couldn't we take phone pics this time and be done with it?"

Jackson didn't seem to have heard her. "They

wouldn't guard it so closely if there weren't something there."

Iris nodded, grappling with both excitement and fear. "Aren't we pushing our luck?" she cautioned. "We've had so many close calls."

Looking grim, Jackson said, "I know. But we can't stop now. We're too close."

SIX

The pre-dawn chill clung to Sleepy Hollow, with wisps of fog curling around the base of ancient trees and weathered tombstones. Iris pulled her jacket tighter as she and Jackson made their way through the silent streets. The town seemed frozen in time, the modern world held at bay by the ethereal mist and looming shadows of colonial-era buildings.

"Are you sure about this?" Iris whispered, her breath visible in the cold air.

Jackson nodded, his face set with determination. In the dim light, his features seemed more angular, almost haunted.

They approached the hidden entrance near the old church, a silent sentinel guarding centuries of secrets.

Jackson moved aside the concealing bush, revealing the opening. "Ready?"

Iris took a deep breath, steeling herself. The musty

scent of earth and old stone wafted from the entrance. "As I'll ever be."

They clicked on their headlamps. The beams cut through the darkness like knives as they descended into the tunnel. The temperature dropped, but this time, Iris was prepared with extra layers of clothing. Oppressive silence engulfed them, broken only by their cautious footsteps and the occasional drip of water from unseen crevices.

"Look at these support beams," Jackson murmured, running his hand along a beam that was lighter than most of the others. His voice, although quiet, echoed in the stony confines. "These tunnels are old, but they've been maintained. Someone's been down here, and not just recently. Notice the varying shades of the wood."

Iris nodded, her historian's mind already cataloging details. She ran her fingers along the wall, feeling the texture of stones that had been in place since before the nation was born. "You can almost imagine the people down here transporting war supplies—or even smuggling goods—during the Revolutionary War. And it probably looked just like this."

As they pressed on, the tunnel gradually widened. Iris noticed markings on the walls that looked vaguely familiar. Her heart quickened when she recognized the pattern.

"Jackson," she called softly, "do you see these? They look like the symbols from the cipher."

Jackson examined the markings closely; his brow furrowed in concentration. "It's like a map, or maybe directions. The Wardens might have used these to navigate the tunnels."

As they followed the symbols, the tunnel began to branch off in multiple directions. Each fork presented a new mystery, a new potential path to unraveling Sleepy Hollow's secrets. They chose a path that seemed to lead deeper underground, the air growing cooler and damper with each step.

Iris's mind wandered to the generations of Wardens who had walked these same paths, carrying with them the weight of their duty. What had they felt, knowing they were guardians of a secret so profound it could shape the destiny of a nation?

Jackson stopped short, causing Iris to bump into him. The warmth of his body was a stark contrast to the chill of the tunnel. "Listen," he whispered, his voice barely audible.

Iris held her breath, listening intently. At first, she heard nothing but the faint drip of water and the pounding of her own heart. Then, barely audible, came the sound of stone scraping against stone.

"Someone else is down here," Jackson whispered, his voice edged with tension.

They quickly doused their headlamps, plunging the tunnel into darkness—so much for their plan to arrive undetected. The place had to be constantly guarded for this to happen again. But why?

Iris felt Jackson's hand find hers, a reassuring touch in the cold blackness. They pressed their backs to the wall, hardly daring to breathe.

The scraping grew louder, accompanied by muffled voices. Iris strained to make out words, but the echoes in the tunnel distorted the sound, transforming it into an eerie, unintelligible murmur.

A faint light appeared around a bend in the tunnel. As it grew brighter, Iris's heart hammered in her chest. Two figures came into view. She recognized one even in the dim light of the flashlights they carried.

Dr. Grice.

The other was a stranger, a tall man with angular features that seemed carved from the same stone as the tunnel walls.

The stranger spoke in a low, raspy voice. "They wouldn't have gone to such lengths to protect an empty chamber. The seal must be down here somewhere."

Grice nodded, his flashlight beam sweeping the walls. "The symbols should lead the way—if we decipher them correctly."

As the men moved past their hiding spot, Iris felt Jackson tense beside her. She tightened her grip on his hand as the seconds stretched into eternity. Frozen in place, they could only wait and hope the intruders would pass.

Once the footsteps faded into the distance, Jackson and Iris let out a collective breath. The tension slowly ebbed from their bodies, leaving behind a mixture of relief and excitement.

"That was too close," Iris whispered, her voice shaky.

"But informative," Jackson replied, a hint of excitement creeping into his tone. "Now we know what they're looking for—a seal. And they think it's hidden down here."

Iris frowned, piecing together the information. "Something doesn't add up. If the Wardens are supposed to protect the Seal, then they'd already know where it was, which Grice clearly doesn't."

Jackson nodded slowly. "You're right. Either the Wardens have changed their mission drastically, or—"

"Or Grice isn't working for them." As Iris finished the thought, a new possibility dawned on her. "Which explains why he's after us."

"Because we're after the same thing, and he's hell-bent on getting there first." Jackson glanced down the tunnel. "Come on. Let's get out of here."

The pair cautiously retraced their steps and emerged from the tunnel as the first rays of sunlight peeked over the horizon. The quiet streets of Sleepy Hollow felt surreal after the near miss they'd had underground. Before them, the fog lifted slowly to reveal a town coming to life. And no one seemed aware of the secrets that lurked there.

As they drove back to the cottage, Iris's mind raced with questions. The cool morning air cleared her head, but each answer spawned a dozen new questions. "What sort of seals did they use back then? And why would anyone care?"

Jackson shook his head, his expression thoughtful. "I'm not sure. There's no mention of a seal in my great-great-grandfather's letters, but they mention a covenant.

Maybe the seal is related to that. I don't know. If there's a connection, we're missing a link. All I have is my gut feeling."

Back at the cottage, the morning sun streamed through the windows as they spread out their notes and the documents from Alexander Wilde's box. They pored over the materials, searching for any mention of a seal. For much of the morning, the only sounds were the rustle of papers, and the occasional gasp followed by a disappointed sigh.

"Here," Iris said suddenly, pointing to a passage in one of the old letters. Her finger trembled as she traced the faded ink. "It mentions a 'sacred seal, guardian of our highest ideals.' Could this be what they're looking for?" But she already knew the answer.

Jackson leaned in, reading the passage. His eyes widened as he absorbed the information. "It has to be. But that doesn't explain what it is or what it is guarding —other than their highest ideals, which tells us nothing."

"Except that it's real."

Jackson shook his head slowly. "And why hide it underground?"

As they continued their research, a pattern emerged. The seal, whatever it was, seemed to be tied to the very foundations of American democracy. References to liberty, justice, and the "true spirit of the Revolution" appeared repeatedly in connection with the mysterious object.

Iris sat back, her mind whirling with possibilities. "I

think," she said slowly, the pieces falling into place, "that this seal might be more than just an object. What if it's a symbol—an ideal—that embodies the core principles the Founding Fathers wanted to protect?"

Jackson nodded, excitement building in his voice. "What you're saying makes sense, but we can't ignore the tunnels."

Fat chance of that! Iris thought of the cobwebs she'd pulled out of her hair.

Jackson went on. "Which is not to say that you're wrong, just that there has to be something tangible along with it. Something that, in the wrong hands, could be used to manipulate those ideals. Which brings us back to the Wardens."

Iris squinted into the distance and nodded. "And what they've protected for so long. So the Seal has to be a physical object."

"And it's in one of those chambers," Jackson said, determination in his eyes.

Iris met his gaze; her excitement tinged with apprehension. "I agree, but—every time we go into those tunnels, there's somebody there. We're not the only ones looking, so..."

"So... we need to find that seal before Grice and his associates do."

Iris searched for words. "Because if we fail—"

"The secret dies with us."

Iris winced. "Well, I wouldn't put it exactly that way."

Jackson's eyes softened. "I'm sorry. Sometimes,

when I latch onto a thought, I forget to be tactful." He reached out and pulled her into his arms.

While his embrace had some pretty amazing healing powers, the truth was, there was no tactful way to spin it. Whatever they did now would lead them further into danger, which was terrifying. But that wasn't the most astonishing aspect of their current situation. Whatever it took, she would do it with him—not for her deep abiding love of history, although that played a part. But being with Jackson—being a part of something greater than the sum of their parts—was important. Their work mattered. And as large as that was, Jackson mattered even more.

Jackson stood, stretching muscles stiff from hours of research. "We should take another look at the cipher," he said, moving to retrieve the document from his bag. "After seeing those symbols in the tunnel, maybe we'll see something we've missed."

As he reached into the bag, his hand brushed against something cold and metallic. Frowning, he pulled out an object—a large coin tarnished with age.

"Iris," he called, his voice tight with excitement. "Look at this."

Iris moved closer, examining the coin. On one side was an intricate design—a seal surrounded by thirteen stars. On the other, a single word: "Libertas."

"Liberty," Iris breathed, her eyes wide. "Jackson, where did you get this?"

Jackson shook his head, turning the coin over in his

hands. "I don't know. It was in my bag, but I've never seen this before."

A chill ran down Iris's spine.

The room seemed to grow colder as they stared at the coin.

Jackson pulled out his phone and took a picture of it, then fired off a text to his research assistant. "Arjun, see what you can learn about this."

Meanwhile, outside, the sun continued to rise over Sleepy Hollow, oblivious to the secrets stirring beneath its tranquil surface.

SEVEN

The afternoon sun filtered through the cottage windows onto the scattered papers and open books that covered every available surface. Iris sat cross-legged on the floor, surrounded by stacks of historical documents, while Jackson paced the room, the newly discovered coin turning over and over in his fingers.

"It just doesn't make sense," he muttered, pausing to examine the coin for the hundredth time. "How did this end up in my satchel? And why now?"

Iris looked up from the letter she'd been studying, feeling tired but determined. "Maybe it's not about the 'why now' but the 'why us.' Someone clearly wanted you to have it."

Before Jackson could respond, a frantic knocking at the door startled them both. They exchanged wary glances. All Iris could think of was Grice and his men.

"Stay here," Jackson whispered, moving cautiously towards the door while Iris searched for something to defend herself with. She glanced at the fireplace and cursed softly. *Gas fireplace. No poker.*

She was on her way to the kitchen knife drawer when Jackson peered through the peephole. "What the hell?"

He swung the door open to reveal a disheveled young man with a backpack slung over one shoulder and a wild look in his eyes.

"Arjun?" Jackson exclaimed. "What are you doing here?"

Arjun Desai stumbled into the cottage, adjusting his crooked glasses, the dark rim tilted just slightly askew on the bridge of his nose. His face was sharply angular, with the hint of a five o'clock shadow along his jawline, but the first thing Iris noticed was the bruise blooming on his right cheek. It wasn't fully developed yet—just a smudge of purple under his tan skin—but it gave him a hardened edge that seemed out of place with the rest of his appearance. His dark, neatly cut hair was ruffled, and his collared shirt had come untucked on one side. Despite his disheveled appearance, there was something undeniably appealing about him. His eyes, though hidden behind the thick lenses, were sharp and alert, scanning the room with an astuteness that belied the awkward position he found himself in.

"Professor Wilde," he gasped, "I'm sorry to just show up like this, but something happened. I didn't know where else to go."

Recognizing the name of Jackson's research

assistant, Iris approached. "Are you okay? Can I get you some water?"

Arjun nodded as Jackson guided the young man to a chair. "What happened?"

Arjun took a shaky breath. "I was at the library, looking into that coin you sent me a picture of. And I found something. I got into the zone researching, and I guess I didn't notice anyone else around me. But when I left, these two guys followed me. I thought I might be imagining things, but when I reached the bodega around the corner from my apartment, they pulled me into an alley and asked—well, demanded to know—what I knew about the Wardens."

Iris and Jackson exchanged concerned looks. Their investigation had just taken a dangerous turn, and now an innocent grad student was caught in the crossfire.

"When I said I didn't know anything—repeatedly—they did this." He gestured to his bruised face. "Repeatedly."

Iris said, "I'm glad you're here. But how did you find us?"

Arjun said, "Oh. I house-sat for Jackson."

Jackson added, "Last semester, when I was on sabbatical."

Iris brought Arjun a glass of water and some ice in a washcloth. After thanking her, Arjun turned to Jackson. "I'm sorry. I was afraid they might know where I live. My apartment's practically next door to the bodega." He shrugged. "I was scared, so I hopped on the next

Hudson line train from 125th Street and got off at Phillipse Manor."

Iris said, "Oh, wow. But how did they know to find you?"

Arjun shook his head.

Increasingly troubled, Iris said, "I just don't understand the connection. Why would they follow you?"

Jackson cursed. "I think I know why."

Arjun's eyes lit up with a mix of fear and excitement. "Your text!"

Jackson cursed. "Arjun, your phone."

Arjun nodded as though he understood, but Iris didn't. "Hello? What's going on?"

Jackson said, "There's a good chance they've hacked one or both of our phones."

Arjun held out his hand. "I've already taken care of mine, but give me your phone. Yours, too, Iris, just in case."

While Arjun removed the SIM cards from the phones and returned them, Jackson ran a hand through his hair and paced for a bit. "Arjun, what else did they ask you? The ones who attacked you?"

The young man's excitement dimmed, replaced by a flicker of fear. "They wanted to know where the coin was."

Iris shot an alarmed look at Jackson.

"And what did you tell them?" Jackson asked.

Arjun shook his head emphatically. "I told them I didn't know—that it came up in some research, but I'd never seen it in person." He gestured toward his bruised face. "Apparently, they didn't believe me at first."

Arjun tilted his head. "But, eventually—after they beat the crap out of me—they gave up and left me in the alley."

Iris was filled with compassion. The poor guy had had quite a day.

Jackson pulled the coin from his pocket and set it down on the table beside Arjun's phone. "So, what did you find out about this?"

Arjun started to reach into his backpack. "Oh, I forgot. They stole my laptop."

"Oh, no! The research!" Jackson looked as distressed as Iris had ever seen him.

"No worries. I erased it remotely." Arjun quickly added, "It's okay. Everything's backed up in the cloud—encrypted, of course."

Jackson's eyes narrowed. "But if they stole your laptop, why wouldn't they take your phone?"

Arjun lifted a palm. "I know what you're thinking—they left it so they could track me. I thought of that, too. So, after I erased my computer, I pulled the SIM card out of my phone. It's okay. Everything's fine."

Jackson exhaled. "So, the coin...?"

Suddenly, Arjun's phone began to spark, then melted, filling the air with the smell of burned electronics.

"What the—"

"The coin," Arjun said, his eyes wide. "Jackson, look!"

To their astonishment, not only had it melted the phone, but now it was glowing and pulsing with energy.

Jackson stared. The coin's otherworldly glow defied explanation. Iris was well aware of how much Jackson prided himself on his rational approach to history, but this had to be challenging everything he thought he knew.

"There has to be a logical explanation," he insisted, more to himself than to Iris.

Iris struggled to comprehend what she was seeing. "Logical or not, it's affecting the electronics."

"And my yogurt spoon," Arjun added. His eyes shone with urgency. "The spoon's a lost cause, but we need to contain all the tech." With a glance at Iris's confused expression, Arjun said, "We need a Faraday cage."

Jackson looked around the room. "I don't exactly have one of those lying around, Arjun."

But Arjun was already moving, his earlier fear replaced by determined focus. "We can make one. Have you got some aluminum foil?"

What? For tin foil hats? Iris resisted the temptation to say it.

Jackson pulled the last twelve inches from a box of foil.

Arjun quickly wrapped the remaining two phones in foil. "Done."

Iris frowned. "We're all out of foil now."

Arjun's eyes darted around. "The microwave. Stack all the tablets and laptops inside." With that accomplished, Arjun said, "Just don't turn it on." He stared at the coin. "We'll need something else for that."

Jackson pulled out his wallet. "Will this work? It's RFID proof."

Arjun nodded. "I mean, we don't know what that coin is, but it's the best we can do for now."

Jackson buried the coin in his wallet.

Meanwhile, Iris was curious—not only about Faraday cages, but about what sorts of metal would behave like that coin.

"Can I have my laptop back now?"

If it's not already fried.

Arjun stared at the microwave. "Yes and no."

"Okay." She trusted Arjun because Jackson trusted him. But she couldn't begin to guess what he was thinking.

Arjun said, "The way all these devices connect, even though it's in the cloud, something could be intercepted. I just think it's safer if we leave them where they are."

"I agree, we need to start from scratch," Jackson said, looking at the electronics. "New devices, off the grid. We can't risk anyone tracking us."

Iris nodded, her mind racing. "And we need to go over everything Arjun found before... this happened."

"Right," Arjun agreed, still looking a bit shell-shocked. "So, before our impromptu light show, I was going to tell you. There are scattered reports of objects with unusual properties, all located along the Eastern seaboard."

Iris narrowed her eyes. "Guys, what else is located along the Eastern seaboard?"

Arjun's eyes lit up. "UAP hotspots?" He glanced from Iris to Jackson. "You know. UFOs?"

After a stunned moment, Iris said, "I was thinking of the original thirteen colonies."

With a strong nod, Arjun said, "Right. Those, too."

His interest piqued, Jackson turned to Arjun. "So, these objects—tell me more."

"Well," Arjun replied. "Let me think. Yeah, there was a compass that points in random directions, a silver eagle figurine that supposedly glows on occasion, and there are rumors of an ornate star with unexplained properties—no details on that. But the fourth one—"

Growing increasingly anxious, Iris said, "Was it—?"

Arjun's eyes darted toward Jackson's wallet. "A coin."

"Where?" Jackson asked, looking somber.

Arjun said softly, "Sleepy Hollow."

<WEDNESDAY EVENING>

WEDNESDAY EVENING

As night fell over Sleepy Hollow, the cottage buzzed with nervous energy. Arjun returned from a quick run to a nearby electronics store, his arms laden with boxes and shopping bags.

"Okay," he said, spreading his purchases across the dining table. "We've got three cheap laptops, three burner phones, and enough parts to build a decent system for analysis." He set down a five-dollar bill and some coins on the table. "Here's your change."

As Arjun set up the equipment, Iris noticed a small Bitcoin logo sticker on his laptop. "You're into crypto?" she asked.

Arjun's eyes lit up. "Oh yeah, I used to mine it in my undergrad dorm room. It's fascinating stuff. The potential applications of blockchain technology are endless. Maybe someday it'll revolutionize how we handle historical artifacts, too."

Jackson chuckled. "Let's focus on the task at hand for now."

Iris and Jackson watched in amazement. His fingers flew over the keyboards, installing software and setting up security measures.

"VPNs on everything," he muttered, more to himself than to them. "And... there. Kill switches installed. If these detect any suspicious activity, they'll wipe themselves clean."

"Impressive," Iris said. "But how does this help us learn about the Wardens?"

Arjun's grin turned mischievous. "We're going to the dark web."

For the next hour, they huddled around the laptops, diving into the murky depths of the internet. Most of what they found was nonsense—conspiracy theories, wild speculation, and the occasional piece of Warden fan fiction that made Jackson cringe.

"Wait," Iris said suddenly, pointing at a thread on one of the forums. "Look at this."

The post detailed a series of unusual property acquisitions across the country. "If I'm not mistaken, these line up with some locations mentioned in the old Warden documents," Jackson realized.

Arjun nodded, already typing furiously. "And look at this—there are mentions of a splinter group. They call themselves 'The Collective' or something."

As they dug deeper, a clearer picture began to emerge. The Wardens of Liberty had indeed fractured, with some members pushing for more direct intervention in politics and others wanting to maintain their traditional role.

Iris's eyes widened as she scanned the forum. "Jackson, look at this. They're talking about something called the 'Founders' Seal.' Apparently, it's some kind of artifact. I'm guessing it must be like a monarch's seal. Whatever it is, the Seal was disassembled—not sure when—and the parts were distributed among different people or maybe groups. It's not clear."

Jackson looked as confused as Iris.

"What else does it say?"

"Not much," Iris admitted. "But there are rumors that different factions are after the pieces. Maybe for protection or power? No one seems to agree." As she considered the new information, it began to make sense. "And if the Wardens are supposed to be protecting these pieces..."

"Then the group that's broken away might be trying to gather them all," Jackson finished. "But for what purpose?"

Just then, one of Arjun's kill switches activated, and the screen went dark. "Someone was probing our connection," he said, his voice tense. "We need to switch networks."

As Arjun worked to secure their connection, Iris and Jackson pored over the information they'd managed to save. The coin, it seemed, was more than just a historical artifact. It was a key to something larger, something the Wardens—and others—were desperate to control.

Jackson started pacing. "Arjun, can you map out the locations of these artifacts?"

Arjun nodded eagerly, fingers flying over his keyboard. "On it."

As Arjun worked, Iris and Jackson continued to sift through the information, looking for patterns or connections. Suddenly, Arjun let out a low whistle.

"Guys, you need to see this," he said, turning his laptop around.

On the screen was a map showing the locations of the artifacts Arjun had found. "I cross-referenced the artifact locations with recent property acquisitions," He then switched to a slide that superimposed recent land purchases where each artifact had been found.

"What?" Jackson leaned closer.

"They match up," Arvis said.

Iris leaned in and pointed. "And they all fall within the thirteen original colonies."

"Jackson leaned back. It's hard to believe it could all be a coincidence."

Iris said, "Property sales and titles are public records, aren't they?"

Arjun said, "I see where you're going with that. I'll just need a few minutes." As his fingers flew over the keyboard, he said, "I'm starving. Got anything to eat?"

Jackson took that as a cue for a break. "Come on, Iris. If we're going to camp out here, we'll need some provisions."

As they headed out the door, Arjun called out as he typed, "I could use some Red Bull and Doritos."

AN HOUR LATER, Jackson and Iris returned from Sam's Club with enough food to last for a couple of weeks.

Arjun's face was lit up. "You are not going to believe this."

Leaving the groceries on the counter, Iris and Jackson pulled up chairs while Arjun filled them in. "It's not easy to find, but there's a pattern here. There are four artifacts. The property where each artifact is rumored to be located was recently purchased. Four artifacts, their four properties, and four companies that bought them. But if you trace the real estate transactions and the purchasing companies—and, believe me, I went through layers and layers of shell corporations to get there—they all lead to one source."

Jackson leaned in closer and read the name on the screen. "The Cassandra Collective?"

Iris squinted. "Cassandra Collective?"

Arjun shrugged. "Greek mythology. She was fated to predict the future, but no one would believe her."

Iris smiled politely. "Yes, I'm aware. But this organization...?"

"Oh. Well, if you believe their website, they're 'on a mission to help families, businesses, and charities make the world better through strategic investing and philanthropy.'" He turned and looked Iris straight in the eye. "But if you dig deeper, there are rumors..."

Arjun popped the tab on a can of Red Bull and grabbed a handful of chips.

"Rumors of what?" Jackson pressed.

After grabbing a napkin to wipe chip dust from his fingers, Arjun said, "That they're actually a dark money political organization," Arjun replied. "But this..." he gestured to the screen, "this suggests they're involved in something bigger. Murky on the details, but a lot of speculation."

"Wait a minute," Iris said, her eyes widening. "The Collective... could this be what Grice is involved with?"

Jackson leaned in, scanning the information. "It's possible. A splinter group from the Wardens, maybe? That would explain why their actions seem to go against everything we know about the Wardens' mission."

Arjun nodded enthusiastically. "It makes sense. Two factions, same knowledge, different goals."

The three of them exchanged looks, the significance of their discovery settling over the room. They had stumbled onto something that looked more extensive and complex than they'd imagined.

"So," Iris said slowly, "we have a mysterious coin with impossible properties and reports of a compass, an eagle figurine, and a star with similar unusual characteristics."

"And a Seal," Arjun added.

Iris nodded. "All rumored to be scattered along the Eastern seaboard, and a shadowy organization that seems to be taking an interest in them."

Jackson nodded grimly. "And somewhere in the middle of all this are the Wardens of Liberty." He paused, a new thought occurring to him. "But the seal and the other artifacts... Exactly how do they fit in?"

The room fell silent for so long Iris startled them both when she said, "How do they fit in? That's it!"

Jackson gave her a doubtful look as if she were slow to catch on. "Yeah... That's what we're trying to figure out."

Iris chuckled. "They fit in because they fit!" She waited for a reaction. "Together."

While Jackson gave it some thought, Arjun blurted out, "Nuclear codes!"

The other two eyed him as though he'd lost his mind. Iris said slowly, "O... kay...."

Arjun looked from Iris to Jackson. "Come on, guys. Keep up. Think about it. It's not like one guy—" His eyes darted to Iris. "Or woman—can just walk around with the red nuke button."

Iris realized Arjun was onto something. She nodded. "It takes more than one person."

"The nuclear football," Jackson said, bright-eyed. "And the card containing the codes that the president carries—the, uh..."

"Biscuit," Arjun's face brightened. "Oh, did you get any cookies?"

He got up and went to the kitchen.

Jackson stared off into space in amazement. "Because power like that shouldn't be in one person's hands."

"Exactly," Arjun added as he returned to his computer, munching on a cookie.

Iris grew troubled. "Judging from that coin, there's some kind of power there. But if the other three parts all have similar powers, and they all fit together, there you have it. The parts *are* the seal—like a king or queen's seal in the olden days."

Jackson raised an eyebrow. "Olden days, like Revolutionary War days?"

"Yes." The thought took Iris's breath away for a moment. "What if the parts are a failsafe? As long as they're kept apart, no one can wield the power of the seal. But if they're brought together—who knows what kind of power it has—power the holder would wield?"

Jackson pushed his hair from his forehead. "It sounds pretty farfetched." He glanced up at Arjun. "Except... one organization has bought up those four tracts of land where the artifacts are."

With a knowing nod, Arjun said, "The Cassandra Collective."

EIGHT

S un filtered through the trees to form dappled shadows on the ground as Iris headed out to meet her last tour of the day. She tried to focus on the familiar routine, but her mind kept drifting back to the coin and the revelations of the previous night.

As her tour group gathered, Iris noticed a man standing at the back, his nondescript features almost too perfect in their blandness. She pushed the thought aside, launching into her well-practiced spiel about the town's founding.

Throughout the tour, Iris found her gaze continually drawn to the man at the back. He never asked questions or snapped photos like the other tourists. He just watched.

As they approached the Old Dutch Church, Iris felt her phone vibrate. As she led the group to the next stop on their walking tour, she quickly glanced at her phone. A text from Jackson.

Be careful. Arjun's picked up chatter about a "package in SH." It could be nothing. Be alert.

Iris's heart raced, but she kept her voice steady as she recounted the legend of the Headless Horseman to her group. All the while, she was acutely aware of the man's unwavering gaze.

The tour concluded back at the Heritage Center. As the group dispersed, the mysterious man lingered to study a nearby historical marker. Iris headed straight for her office. Hearing footsteps following behind her, she sped up her pace.

A woman a few feet away helped her young children into her car. Across the parking lot, two college-aged guys with backpacks walked toward the Old Church. She exhaled. There were people around. She was nearing the Center's entrance when a white van pulled up alongside her. The side door slid open, revealing two men with grim expressions. Panic surged through her.

Jackson's voice cut through her fear as he strode towards her with a broad smile that didn't reach his eyes. "There you are! Sorry I'm late, babe," Jackson said loudly as he scanned the area. "Ready for lunch?"

Before Iris could react, Jackson took her hand and playfully ran to a car, where he pulled her into his arms and kissed her so long and so well that, out of the corner of her eye, Iris saw passersby stop and stare. Jackson released Iris in time to watch the man who had followed on foot jump into the van. The door slammed shut, and the van drove away.

Iris was breathless. Adrenalin pumped through her. Her heart raced, and her mind was a befuddling mixture of mental video replays involving the man on the tour, the two men in the van, and the man who had just kissed her. Her knees were still trembling.

Jackson gripped Iris's shoulders. "I got here as fast as I could. Are you okay?" he asked, his voice tense with concern.

Her voice came out in a breathless whisper. "Yes." But in truth, she was reeling from a wild swing of emotions. Two men had just tried to abduct her, and she could still feel Jackson's lips on hers.

As he pulled out of the parking lot, Jackson glanced over at her, his jaw tight. "You're sure you're okay?"

Iris nodded, but her heart still pounded in her chest, the adrenaline from the narrow escape still coursing through her. "That was too close. How did you know?"

"Arjun's been monitoring local communications," Jackson said, keeping his eyes on the road, his hands gripping the steering wheel a little too tightly.

Iris turned toward him, raising her eyebrows. "What's that supposed to mean?"

Jackson sighed, glancing at her before continuing. "He hacked into a few private forums criminals used to communicate. You've heard of Steemit and Minds, right? Blockchain platforms—nearly impossible to trace unless you know what you're doing. They've been using them to pass coded messages."

"And Arjun's watching them?" she asked, incredulous. "I thought those platforms were all about free speech and decentralization, not... criminals."

"Exactly. That's what makes them perfect for it. No central authority to shut anything down. But Arjun—he's good. He flagged some chatter on Steemit this morning. They mentioned a package pickup at the Heritage Center. I didn't think they'd act this fast, though."

Iris leaned back, processing this new information. Blockchain platforms, criminal forums, coded messages—it all sounded like something out of a spy movie, but here they were, right in the middle of it.

As they drove, Iris filled Jackson in on the suspicious man from her tour. "They're getting bolder," she said, still feeling shaky.

THEY ARRIVED at Jackson's cottage and walked in to find Arjun in the corner at the makeshift command station he'd set up using two folding tables and an impressive array of computer screens and tech gear.

"You're okay!" Arjun exclaimed as they entered. "I was worried when I lost visual on you."

Iris raised an eyebrow. "You had a visual?"

Arjun had the decency to look sheepish. "Hacked the town's traffic cams. For safety!"

As they settled in, Arjun brought them up to speed on his findings. "I've been digging deeper into those property acquisitions we found last night. The

Cassandra Collective isn't alone. There's chatter about other groups looking for these artifacts, too."

Jackson frowned. "Other groups? Like rival factions?"

Arjun nodded vigorously. "Exactly. It's like there's a whole underground world we've stumbled into. And get this—I found another reference to the 'Founders' Seal' in some seriously encrypted forums."

Iris leaned in, intrigued. "What do they say about it?"

"Nothing concrete," Arjun admitted. "More of the same—talk about gathering the pieces—for protection or power. It doesn't make a whole lot of sense."

Jackson's hand went to his pocket. "Anything about a coin?" he asked softly.

Arjun shrugged. "It's definitely one of the pieces."

Jackson paced. "So, the Wardens are protecting these pieces—from what?"

As they continued to discuss their theories, a ping from one of Arjun's computers interrupted them. "Uh oh," he muttered, his fingers flying over the keyboard. "We've got company. Someone's probing our network."

"Can you block them?" Jackson asked, tension evident in his voice.

Arjun's brow furrowed in concentration. "I'm trying, but they're good. Really good."

Suddenly, the screens went dark. Slowly, a message appeared in a single line of white letters scrolling across the screen.

Arjun sat wide-eyed. "What the heck?"

We know what you seek. The Founders' Seal is not to be trifled with. Meet us at the Sleepy Hollow Lighthouse by midnight if you want answers. If you bring anyone with you, you'll regret it.

As the message faded, Iris, Jackson, and Arjun exchanged worried looks.

When he'd recovered from the shock, Arjun said, "I don't know how they got past my firewall, encryption, VPN—I mean, there's no way."

But they had, and they'd issued a challenge to meet someone who clearly knew more than they did. Now feeling paranoid, Iris went to the window and looked out for any signs of intruders. "Great. So, they've hacked into our computer, they know where I work, and now they want us to meet them so they can—"

"Kill us," Arjun said, his voice barely above a whisper.

"Arjun," Jackson cautioned quietly.

Iris turned to find Jackson looking grim but determined. "No. You're not thinking of going!"

"I am," he said plainly.

"No. Come on, Jackson. They just tried to kidnap me—and God knows what else. And now you're suggesting we just stop by for a chat?"

Jackson took both her hands in his. "Not we—I. The Wardens are my family heritage. I've got to follow this to the end."

"To whose end? Yours? Jackson, this is insane."

"Probably. But I'm going."

There was no use arguing with him. He was determined to go. There was only one thing for Iris to do. "Okay, fine. Then I'm going with you."

That prompted a heated discussion, which was brought to a halt when Arjun dramatically covered his ears and said, "I hate it when mommy and daddy fight!"

Iris and Jackson stopped and turned to see Arjun suppressing a grin.

"Come on, guys. Just figure it out or I'll go."

After a calmer discussion, Jackson relented. The two of them would go while Arjun stayed behind and monitored the meeting through their phone mics. Iris was fine with the plan until a thought occurred to her. "But won't they want all of us there so they can eliminate all the witnesses?" She added, "Sorry, Arjun."

Arjun pulled off his headset. "They don't know I'm here."

Iris wasn't convinced. "They knew you were there when they dragged you into a dark alley."

"It was daylight, but I get your point. But as far as they know, I'm an uninformed research assistant—one harmless enough to leave in that alley."

Iris shook her head. "They hacked into your computer, so they must think you know something."

Arjun smiled. "They didn't hack through this." He pointed to a piece of black electrical tape that covered the camera lens on the monitor. Then he pointed to the mic plug, where he'd plugged in one end of a cord and cut off the other. "No camera, no mic. It's low-tech, but it works. Trust me, I'm not on their radar."

They proceeded to plan their midnight rendezvous.

With all they were discovering about the mysteries of
Sleepy Hollow, the Wardens, and the Founders' Seal,
Jackson was convinced they had no choice but to go,
and reluctantly, Iris agreed.

In a few hours, they would have answers to at least
some of their questions. Whether they would survive
after that was another matter.

NINE

The Sleepy Hollow Lighthouse stood sentinel
over the Hudson River, its beam cutting through
the misty night air. Iris checked her watch: 11:45 PM.
In fifteen minutes, they would potentially come face-to-
face with someone who knew far more about the
Founders' Seal than they did.

"I still think it's a trap," Arjun's voice crackled
through their earpieces. He was parked a safe distance
away, monitoring the situation through an array of
surveillance equipment he'd cobbled together.

"Noted," Jackson replied, his eyes scanning the
shoreline. "But we need answers, and this might be our
only chance to get them."

Iris nodded, though her stomach churned with a
mixture of anticipation and dread. "Let's go over the
plan one more time."

"We approach together," Jackson said. "If anything
feels off, we get out immediately. Arjun, you're our eyes

and ears. Any sign of trouble, you alert us and call the police."

"Got it," Arjun confirmed. "Be careful, guys."

As they made their way over the bridge to the lighthouse, the water that lapped against the bridge seemed unnaturally loud. The door at the base was slightly ajar, sending a sliver of light spilling onto the gangway.

Jackson placed a hand on Iris's arm, his touch sending an involuntary shiver through her that had nothing to do with the cool night air. "Ready?"

She nodded, steeling herself.

With an ominous creak from the old wooden door, they stepped inside the lighthouse. The interior was dimly lit by a lantern that cast flickering shadows along the curved walls. A spiral staircase wound its way toward the top and disappeared into darkness.

"Up here." A voice called down from above, startling them both.

Exchanging a wary glance, Iris and Jackson began to climb. Each echoing step amplified the tension. As they reached the top, they arrived in the lamp room, surrounded by windows that offered a 360-degree view of the Hudson and the surrounding shoreline.

A man stood with his back to them, silhouetted against the massive Fresnel lens that housed the lighthouse's beam. Slowly, he turned to face them.

"Dr. Wilde, Dr. Drake. I'm glad you could make it." The voice belonged to an older man, his face lined with age and what looked like years of worry.

"Who are you?" Jackson demanded, positioning himself slightly in front of Iris.

The man smiled sadly. "I'm an old friend of your father's. My name is Thomas Crane. And yes, before you ask, I am a descendant of Ichabod Crane."

Iris's eyes widened. "But Ichabod Crane was just a character in Irving's story."

Crane shook his head. "Irving served with my ancestor in the Marines. The name must have amused him, but Ichabod wasn't anything like the character in Irving's story. But you're not here to learn about my family tree."

While Iris was relieved that Crane posed no danger, she was confused.

Crane continued. "Along with your father, I've been tasked with protecting a secret far older and more dangerous than any headless horseman."

"The Founders' Seal," Jackson said, his voice barely above a whisper.

Crane nodded. "So, you know of it. I shouldn't be surprised. The Wardens have always attracted bright and inquisitive minds."

"We're not Wardens," Iris clarified. "We're just... historians."

Jackson shot her a puzzling look and then turned back to Crane.

"Ah, but that's how it often starts," Crane replied. "The Seal has a way of calling to those who are meant to protect it. Whether you know it or not, you've already taken the first steps on a path that will change your lives forever."

Jackson exhaled and spoke with an edge to his voice. "Let's cut to the chase. What exactly is the Founders' Seal? And why is the Cassandra Collective so interested in it?"

Crane's expression darkened. "The Seal is a powerful artifact created as a safeguard against tyranny. When assembled, it has the power to... well, let's just say it can be very disarming. But in the wrong hands, it could distort the balance of power and destroy our republic."

"That's impossible," Iris said, her historian's skepticism kicking in.

"Is it?" Crane challenged. "You've had the coin."

"How did you know that?" But as Jackson said it, the answer dawned on him. "Unless... you're the one who slipped it into my satchel." Jackson touched his hand to his wallet containing the coin.

Crane didn't deny it. "You must have seen what just one piece can do. Imagine the power of the whole."

A chill ran through Iris as she remembered the coin's strange effect on electronics.

"As for the Cassandra Collective," Crane continued, "they're a rogue group—former Wardens who believed the nation was on the wrong course, and the Seal was their way to correct it. They think they know better than we, the people."

Realization dawned on Iris's face. "So, it's not the Wardens who've been after us. It's this Collective."

Crane nodded gravely. "The Wardens have been trying to protect the Seal for generations. The Collective broke away, believing they could use its power to reshape the nation according to their own vision."

Jackson's jaw tightened. "And Grice is with them."

"Precisely," Crane confirmed. "The Wardens aren't your enemy here. The Collective is. The founding fathers' vision for government endures to this day through a delicate balance of power. The Cassandra Collective seeks to usurp that power. But they can't do that without the Seal."

Jackson looked deeply troubled. "My father hasn't said a word about any of this. So why am I here?"

"That's a story for another day. Today, we're here for this." He reached into the metal frame under the Fresnel lens and produced a compass. "The final piece of the Seal."

"Why are you telling us this?"

Arjun's voice cut through their earpieces. "Guys, we've got company. Multiple vehicles approaching fast."

Approaching headlights reflected from the lens. Crane turned to the window. "They've found us."

Before they could react, the sound of breaking glass shattered the quiet night. A canister rolled across the floor, spewing thick, acrid smoke.

"Get down!" Jackson yelled, pulling Iris to the floor. "Find the stairs. We've got to get out before—"

Through the haze, Iris saw dark figures swarming up the steps. As one intruder reached the top step,

Crane lunged toward Jackson and pressed the compass into his hand. "Trust the compass to lead you." The next second, a masked intruder struck Crane on the head, and he fell down the stairs. As he fell, a rolled-up paper fell onto the floor.

Iris scrambled to reach for it. Her fingers closed around the edge of what felt like parchment.

"I'll take that," a muffled voice demanded.

She looked up at the cold eyes of a masked assailant staring down at her.

Before Iris could respond, Jackson tackled him, sending them both crashing into the delicate machinery of the lighthouse lamp. A sharp crack sounded. As shattered glass fell to the floor, the beacon broke, plunging the room into darkness.

Iris slipped the parchment into her bra for safe-keeping and felt her way to the stairs. She heard Jackson fighting off the intruder, then silence. She couldn't see through the smoke, let alone breathe.

"Iris, go!"

"Jackson?"

"Go ahead. I'm behind you." As she stumbled down the stairs, a hand from below grabbed her arm. She lashed out instinctively, connecting with something solid.

"Ow! Iris, it's me!" Arjun's voice cut through her panic.

"Arjun? What are you doing here?"

"Getting beat up again," he said, pulling her towards the exit. "Come on, we need to get out of here!"

They burst out of the lighthouse, gulping in the fresh night air. Behind them, they heard the sounds of a struggle still coming from above.

"Where's Crane?" Iris gasped. "Did anyone see him?"

But before they could answer, a figure came flying out of the lighthouse door. Crane staggered into the bridge railing and headed down the bridge, his face streaked with blood.

"Run!" he shouted.

Two figures approached and helped him to a waiting car.

"Go," he shouted again to the three of them.

Arjun, Jackson, and Iris sprinted for the car, the sounds of running footsteps close behind. As they climbed into the SUV, Iris looked back to see two dark-clad figures emerge from the building.

"Everyone here?" Arjun asked as he swerved onto the main road.

"Yeah," Jackson said, his breathing ragged.

"Just taking attendance." Arjun glanced in the mirror as he gripped the wheel.

Jackson said, "Crane handed me a compass. Iris, that rolled-up paper, what was it?"

She reached into her shirt and pulled out a crumpled piece of parchment. "I don't know. But I've got it right here."

Jackson exhaled. "Good."

As they sped away from the lighthouse and Sleepy Hollow, several miles passed in silence, each lost in their thoughts about the night's events. Suddenly, Arjun slammed on the brakes, and the car skidded to a halt.

"What the hell, Arjun?" Jackson exclaimed.

But Arjun was pointing ahead, his eyes wide. "Look!"

In the middle of the road stood a figure, barely visible in the gloom. As they stared, it raised an arm, pointing in the direction they were headed. Then, in a blink, it vanished.

"Uh... please tell me you saw that." Arjun's voice was shaky.

Iris nodded, her throat dry. "It looked like..."

"No," Jackson said firmly. "For one thing, there was no horse."

"And no head," Arjun added with a quivering voice.

Iris didn't want to believe what she'd seen. "How can you tell? It's pitch black out here on the Taconic."

They sat in stunned silence for a moment before Jackson spoke again. "We can't stay here. Arjun, I'll drive."

Arjun gladly relinquished his seat. "Where?"

Jackson slid into the driver's seat. "Anywhere—till we find someplace safe."

As they continued down the dark road, Iris carefully unfolded the parchment she'd snatched from the lighthouse. In the dim light of the car's interior, she could make out what looked like a map of the Eastern seaboard, with several locations detailed.

"Guys," she said softly, "I think this might be a map leading to the other pieces of the Seal."

Jackson glanced over with widening eyes.

"Deer!" Arjun yelled.

Jackson swerved and barely missed a deer as it leaped across the road.

"Eyes on the road," Arjun muttered.

Ignoring him, Jackson said, "If that's real—"

Iris glared at Jackson. "Of course it's real! You know what else feels real? Having strange guys attack us."

Jackson didn't reply, which made Iris feel guilty. "I'm sorry I snapped. I'm a little stressed. All I need is one day of not being chased and assaulted."

Jackson said gently, "We need a safe place to regroup."

Arjun leaned his head back on the headrest. "Well, damn. I gave up the lease to my top-secret safe house when I started grad school."

Iris smiled. "I know what you mean. I can barely afford my apartment on my pay. Oh, crap. Work. I'll have to call in sick."

A slow smile spread across Jackson's face. "I might know a place."

"Nice. But just so you know, we only stay in gazillion-dollar waterfront cottages."

Jackson tossed a weary look toward her. "Well, this is a cabin, so...."

Arjun chimed in, "Well, okay—as long as it's a gazillion-dollar cabin."

Iris shrugged, "We've got standards."

Jackson smiled. "I just need to make a quick phone call to make sure no one's there." He pulled out his phone. "Crap. No signal."

Iris said, "Yeah, well, good luck finding a signal in Westchester."

Twenty minutes down the road, Iris cried, "Signal!"

Jackson slammed on the brakes and pulled off to the side. He cursed at his phone. "Lost it. Hold on." He got out of the car and climbed partway up an embankment.

A minute later, he got back in the car. "We're going to the Adirondacks."

TEN

The Land Rover jolted along the rough Adirondack back road, waking Iris from a restless sleep. The dawn light revealed the rugged wilderness of upstate New York. Thick forests of fir, spruce, and pine trees lined the road, broken only by the occasional glint of still lake water. The air was crisp, with a sharp scent of pine. Iris drew in a breath, and for the first time in days, exhaled with relief. They were safe, for now.

The events of the last few hours replayed in her mind: the lighthouse, the ambush, their narrow escape. It all felt so surreal.

Jackson drove with steady focus, his deep hazel eyes locked on the winding road ahead. In the glow of the early morning light, his sharp features seemed even more defined—angular jaw, a day's worth of stubble, and his dark hair tousled from lack of sleep. The polished, put-together man she'd first met was now rugged, battle-worn—and even more attractive for it.

Her gaze wandered to his hands—strong, capable, gripping the wheel with the same care he'd once used to handle ancient relics. Those same hands that had, in the heat of the moment, cupped her face and pulled her in for a kiss. The memory of it lingered far longer than she wanted to admit. Her heart stirred at the thought, but she quickly suppressed it.

She wanted to believe that the kiss had been more than a ruse. It felt more real than a spur-of-the-moment decision to thwart a kidnapping. Yet, afterward, Jackson had barely acknowledged it, as if it had never happened.

Iris glanced at him again, searching his face for clues. Was it regret that kept him quiet?

She pulled her jacket tighter around her, more from uncertainty than the cold.

"Where are we going?" she asked, breaking the silence that had grown too heavy.

Jackson's grip on the wheel tightened, and for a moment, she wasn't sure if he'd answer. Finally, he glanced at her, his voice steady but distant. "A cabin. We'll be safe there for a while."

Iris frowned. "A cabin? Whose cabin?"

"It's a place my family owns."

"Oh." *Another family property? A cottage in Westchester and a cabin in the Adirondacks? Do they have pied-à-terres conveniently scattered throughout the lower forty-eight?* "You've never mentioned a cabin before."

"There's a lot I haven't mentioned," he replied, his tone flat.

She wasn't sure if that was meant to shut her down or open the door to questions. The uncertainty gnawed at her. In the early days of their research, Jackson had been an open book—warm, approachable, and quick to share his theories and thoughts. Now, with everything at stake, he'd closed off, and she could feel the distance growing between them, like a wall he'd built brick by brick.

The car dipped as they turned onto a narrower gravel road that wound deeper into the woods. Iris pressed her lips together. Being mistrusting and needy had never been her style. She just needed to calm down and focus on the task before them.

Arjun's voice from the back seat broke the silence.

"So, we're going to hide out in the woods?" Arjun sat up, his eyes still bleary from sleep, but his voice was as sharp as ever. "I mean, that's cool. We could all use a break, but shouldn't we be doing something more?"

Jackson glanced at the rearview mirror. "We will. But first, we need to regroup."

Regroup. Iris's stomach twisted. That was all they'd been doing lately, moving from one crisis to another, always on the defensive, never quite sure of the ground beneath their feet. She longed for a moment of stability, but even more than that, she longed for answers.

As they turned a final bend, a cabin came into view.

It was small, nestled against a backdrop of towering pines with a log exterior that blended seamlessly into the forest. The lake beside it reflected the silvery sky, casting a tranquil spell over the scene.

Jackson parked the car and stepped out, taking a deep breath of the mountain air. "We're here."

Iris stepped out of the car, her eyes lingering on Jackson's rigid posture as he surveyed the area. He was keeping something from them, from her. And that secret, whatever it was, had started to gnaw at her trust.

She shook off the feeling. There would be time to talk later, or so she hoped. For now, they needed to settle in.

Arjun yawned and stretched, climbing out of the backseat. "So, what's the plan? Food, sleep, then try not to get killed?"

Jackson pulled something out of his pocket. "See what you can find out about this and Iris's map."

Arjun took it and turned it over. "Looks like a compass."

"Yeah, but Crane gave it to me, so my guess is it's part of the Seal."

They unpacked quickly, securing their things inside the cabin. It was cozy and well-stocked with supplies that looked like they'd been there for years. Jackson moved with practiced ease, knowing where everything was as if he'd been here countless times before. Meanwhile, Arjun explored the space with his usual curiosity, marveling at the old books on the shelves and tinkering with the radio equipment he'd dusted off in a corner.

Iris stayed by the window, watching the lake's still surface, but the peace of the setting did little to calm her unease. Her thoughts kept circling back to Jackson. She was making too much of it. They were working together. That's all. If there was an attraction, his feelings had cooled, so now it was back to business as usual.

"Hey," his voice came from behind her, soft but with that same distance that had settled between them.

She turned, her heart quickening, but she kept her voice calm. "Hi."

"You okay?"

Iris offered a tight smile. "Yeah. Just... thinking."

Jackson's brow furrowed, but before he could say anything, Arjun popped his head into the room. "So, Jackson—about that compass. You were right. It's some kind of weird Warden tech. Because when I was messing with it earlier... well, let's just say it did things that regular compasses don't do."

Jackson straightened. "Let me see."

Arjun handed the compass to him, and Iris watched as Jackson's entire demeanor shifted. He examined it closely, turning it over in his hands, but there was something guarded about the way he did it.

"I'm sure Crane gave it to us for a reason," Arjun continued, oblivious to the tension building in the room. "I'm just wondering why."

Jackson nodded absently, his focus still on the compass, and Iris's chest tightened. He was withdrawing again, slipping into whatever secret world he was keeping locked away.

She stepped closer, unable to keep the question bottled up any longer. "What aren't you telling us, Jackson?"

He blinked, clearly caught off guard by her directness. "What do you mean?"

"You've been... different ever since the lighthouse. Distant. Like there's something else we don't know."

Jackson met her gaze, but the wall between them held firm. He opened his mouth to respond, but then seemed to think better of it and looked away instead. "I'm just trying to keep us safe."

"You know what would make me feel safe? Facts." Iris pressed, frustration creeping into her voice. "That would be helpful."

"Iris." Jackson's voice was low, his eyes dark as they met hers. "There are things... I can't explain right now. Not until I'm sure."

"Sure of what?" she asked, her heart sinking with the realization that he wasn't going to give her a straight answer.

Jackson ran a hand through his hair, clearly torn, but before he could respond, Arjun's phone buzzed loudly, breaking the tension.

"Uh... We've got a situation," Arjun said, his tone shifting from casual to serious as he scanned the screen. "Looks like we weren't as hard to find as we thought. Someone's pinging our location."

Jackson swore under his breath, already moving toward the door. "Pack your things. We can't stay."

Iris hesitated, her frustration with Jackson still burning, but she caught herself before she reacted. Instead of letting it cloud her judgment, she focused on the present.

"Wait!" Eyes glued to his laptop, Arjun tapped frantically at the keys. "It's okay. They didn't hack in, but they got close. I'll just scramble our coordinates and give them a few decoys to chase while we stay off the grid."

Jackson paused with his hand on the doorknob and watched Arjun work. "How much time will that buy us?"

"Hard to say," Arjun replied, his fingers flying over the keyboard. "Could be hours, could be minutes, depending on how good they are at hacking. But I've rerouted the signal through a few different servers. For now, we're ghosts." He grinned, a hint of pride in his voice. "They'll be chasing shadows."

Jackson exhaled, the tension easing from his shoulders. "Good work. Let me know the second anything changes."

"Already on it." Arjun set up his laptop on the kitchen table, screens popping up as he monitored different feeds. "I'll keep an eye on their movements."

Iris felt the rush of adrenaline fade slightly, the urgency replaced by a quieter tension. She turned to Jackson, who was watching Arjun with an unreadable expression.

For now, they were safe.

Jackson caught her looking at him, and for a brief second, something in his eyes softened. The tension between them had been simmering ever since their kiss, and now, standing in the stillness of the cabin, it felt like the air between them was thick with unspoken words.

"You should get some rest while you can," Jackson said finally, his voice low, but it lacked the sharpness of before.

"Right," Iris agreed, her heartbeat still unsettled, but her voice calm. "You too."

Jackson nodded and disappeared into one of the small bedrooms, leaving Iris standing there, unsure of what to feel.

She walked over to Arjun, who was fully engrossed in the computer. "How's it looking?"

"For now, we're okay," he said without looking up. "I've set up a few different traps for them to chase, but I'm keeping watch in case they catch on." He paused for a second, then grinned at her. "This would be kind of fun if they weren't trying to kill us."

Iris smiled. "You and I have entirely different ideas of fun."

Arjun grinned, but his eyes darted briefly to the bedroom Jackson had just entered. "So, what's up with you two?"

She hesitated, then gave a slight shrug. "Us? Nothing. Just tired."

Arjun raised an eyebrow, then turned to focus on his screen.

Iris wandered back to the porch, the cool night air a welcome contrast to the heavy atmosphere inside the cabin. She let the quiet of the still lake wash over her. Whatever was happening with Jackson—whatever secrets he was holding—she couldn't let it distract her. There was too much at stake.

Which sounded so sensible, until the memory of his lips on hers destroyed her resolve. And the way he'd pulled back afterward—it wasn't just the kiss, it was everything. It was like he was shielding her from something, holding her at arm's length for reasons she couldn't understand.

Footsteps from behind interrupted her thoughts. She turned to see Jackson standing there, hands shoved into his jacket pockets, his expression softer than it had been all day.

"Couldn't sleep?" he asked, his voice quiet.

"No, I just needed some air," Iris replied, leaning against the porch railing. "You?"

Jackson joined her at the railing, his shoulder brushing hers, and for a moment, neither of them spoke. The tension between them, unspoken and palpable, hung in the air.

"You were right," he said suddenly, his voice low. "Earlier. I know I've been... distant."

Iris glanced at him, surprised at the sudden admission. "It's okay," she said. *Well, that's a frigging lie.* "There's a lot going on."

Jackson shook his head. "No, it's more than that. I've been keeping things from you. Not because I don't trust you, but because... I don't know what it all means yet. And until I do, I don't want to... complicate things."

Iris's chest tightened, but she kept her voice steady. "Jackson, you've lost me."

Jackson hesitated, his eyes searching hers. "There's more to all of this. To the compass, to the Founders' Seal, and to my family's role in it. I've been trying to figure it out, but I don't have all the answers yet. And until I do, I didn't want to drag you into it."

Iris's heart pounded, the pieces of the puzzle clicking into place.

That's it? Because now I'm more confused than ever.

She didn't want to argue or pry—or assume feelings that weren't ever there. But hers were.

Jackson met her gaze with a conflicted expression. "I didn't want to make promises I couldn't keep. Not until I knew what I was dealing with."

"Promises?" *I haven't asked for... anything. Except maybe honesty.*

And then the implication behind his words sank in. Frustration and hurt gave way to understanding. He wasn't keeping her out because he didn't care—he was trying to protect her.

"Jackson," she said softly, stepping closer. "I'm not asking for anything except honesty. Just don't shut me out."

His eyes softened, and for a moment, the tension between them melted away. He reached up, brushed a strand of hair behind her ear, and his fingers lingered on her cheek. "I don't want to shut you out."

Then, as if drawn by an unspoken pull, he leaned in, his lips brushing hers. This time, the kiss wasn't a strategy or necessity—it was real, tender, and full of everything that hadn't been said.

When they finally parted, Jackson rested his forehead against hers, his voice barely above a whisper. "We'll figure it out."

Iris nodded, her heart still racing from the kiss, but the doubt that had been gnawing at her began to fade.

Just as the moment between them began to settle, Arjun's voice broke through the quiet, sharp with tension. "Uh, guys?"

They turned to see him in the doorway, laptop in hand, his expression tight with concern. "I hate to interrupt, but... someone's trying to track us. The decoy held them off for a while, but they've breached our first layer of security." He sat down in a porch chair and typed. Jackson's face darkened as the familiar urgency returned. "How long do we have?"

Arjun's fingers flew across the keys. "Not long if I don't move fast—give me a minute."

Iris felt the warmth of the moment between her and Jackson evaporate, replaced by the cold reality that they were still being hunted.

For a few agonizing seconds, the only sound was the furious clicking of Arjun's keyboard. He muttered under his breath, his eyes scanning the screen with laser focus. Then he heaved a deep breath and leaned back in his chair. "Okay, I've rerouted the signal and set up a new decoy. We're clear for now, but they got closer than I'd like."

Jackson exhaled, his grip loosening on Iris's hand. "You're sure we're good?"

"For now," Arjun confirmed, though his gaze stayed on the screen. "I'll keep monitoring. But we should probably leave in the morning."

The shadow of danger loomed close. Iris met Jackson's eyes, feeling the impact of what almost happened.

"We'll stay for now," Jackson said, his tone measured, "but we have to be ready."

ELEVEN

The cabin settled into a tense quiet after the close call with the cyber intruders. Iris and Jackson moved carefully around each other, their earlier argument still hanging in the air, not entirely unresolved but shelved.

Overnight, they took turns keeping watch. By dawn, Jackson had taken up a post by the window while Arjun alternated between scooping spoonfuls of cereal and typing furiously at his laptop. He had managed to divert the threat through the night, but the atmosphere remained charged.

Iris sat up on the couch where she'd fallen asleep, her thoughts swirling between Jackson's sudden withdrawal and the larger mystery that still weighed heavily on them. She could hear the soft, rhythmic clacking of Arjun's keys, a calming rhythm against the background of tension. She didn't want to think too hard about Jackson right now. There was too much else at stake.

"Uh, you guys might want to come over here for a second," Arjun called out, his tone laced with more surprise.

Jackson moved immediately, as if expecting bad news. Iris followed, her curiosity piqued by Arjun's uncharacteristically uncertain voice.

"What did you find?" Jackson asked, stepping around the cluttered table to peer at Arjun's screen.

Arjun turned the laptop toward them, pointing at the compass Crane had given them, which was now scanned into a decryption program. On his screen, a faded map was slowly materializing from the cryptic coordinates and symbols they'd been puzzling over.

"I think this is what Crane was getting at before..." Arjun paused, choosing his words carefully, "before things went sideways at the lighthouse. I decrypted the map from the marks on the compass. Look at this."

Iris leaned in, her breath catching as she recognized the area on the map. "That's Sleepy Hollow. Right there."

Jackson nodded, narrowing his eyes at a mark on the map. "What's this?" He pointed to a large estate sketched into the outline of the region.

Arjun tapped a few keys, bringing the estate into clearer focus. "According to Crane's data, this estate belonged to one of his ancestors, and from what I'm reading here, it's the last known location tied to the Founders' Seal."

"The estate," Iris whispered, tracing the location with her finger. She could almost feel the history, the implications of it pressing against her. "And what about this mark here? That's the church."

Jackson straightened, eyes locked on the map. "Two marks. Two missing pieces," he answered, his voice firm. "That's what we need to complete this."

Arjun sat back, folding his arms, clearly pleased with himself. "You're looking at our next two stops. If this map is accurate, that estate is holding what we're missing."

"And Crane knew it," Iris said softly. "He wanted us to find and protect them, but why?"

A quiet chill ran through her as the enormity of the discovery settled in. After everything they had been through—the coin, the compass, the constant danger, and the unanswered questions—they were finally close to something real. Something that could change everything.

"Do we have any idea what we're looking for, exactly?" Jackson asked.

"No specifics yet," Arjun admitted, "but the map references a vault in a hidden underground chamber. And over here, at his family's estate, Crane said it would be hiding in plain sight."

Jackson rubbed his jaw, lost in thought. "I'm guessing the final piece is there. If I were guarding the Seal, I'd want the last piece closest to me."

Iris agreed. "So, we have one more go at the underground tunnels. We've obviously missed something there."

"And then the Crane estate." Jackson met Iris's

eyes, and this time, there was no distance between them. Only shared purpose.

Arjun swiveled back to his screen. "I'll dig into the estate's security to make sure we can clear it."

Iris nodded, her heart racing in anticipation. Finally, they had a direction, a concrete lead that would bring them closer to uncovering the Founders' Seal and, hopefully, the truth Crane was trying to tell them.

"Arjun, how long will it take you to get us everything we need on this estate?" Jackson asked, his tone all business now.

"Give me a couple of hours," Arjun said, already immersed in data. "I'll get us past the digital walls. We just have to hope no one else is trying to break in at the same time."

Iris felt a spark of determination. They'd come this far, and now they had the map to guide them the rest of the way. All they had to do was stay ahead of the Collective.

But as she sat back, her fingers brushing the edge of the decrypted map, she thought about the new danger ahead. Sleepy Hollow was no longer just the place where their adventure had begun—it was now the key to unlocking everything. And it appeared everyone else hunting for the Seal knew it, too.

Hours passed, and Arjun was buried deep in his work, hacking into the estate's security system and retrieving blueprints of the property. Jackson had resumed his quiet patrol of the perimeter, the tension in his shoulders unmistakable. Iris tried to relax, but her thoughts kept turning to the estate, to Crane, and to Jackson's increasing silence since the lighthouse.

Finally, Arjun called them over once again, a new gleam in his eye.

"Okay, I've got us a full layout of the estate. The good news is we've got a way in without raising too many alarms. The bad news is..."

He paused, glancing at the screen.

"What?" Jackson pressed, his expression hardening.

Arjun tapped the keyboard, bringing up a set of red flashing alerts on his screen. "The Collective's getting close. I diverted the ping earlier, but they're persistent. They're trying new methods. I'm holding them off for now, but we've got to move."

Iris's pulse quickened. "Are we being tracked?"

"Not yet," Arjun said, tapping furiously on the keys. "But they're getting more aggressive. I'll buy us some time, but we can't stay here much longer. They'll eventually hack through the system, and then we'll have nowhere to hide."

Jackson cursed under his breath. "How long?"

"A few more hours—tops," Arjun replied. "But once they break through, they'll know exactly where we are. We'll need to be on the road by then."

Iris exchanged a glance with Jackson. They had only a tiny window before everything went south.

"We leave tonight," Jackson said, the finality in his voice unmistakable.

Arjun nodded, already packing up his gear. "I'll monitor from the road. We'll need to be ready for anything."

Iris grabbed her jacket and glanced back at Jackson. He was focused, intense, and for the first time in days, they seemed completely in sync.

TWELVE

T he moon was hovering high in the sky by the time Iris, Jackson, and Arjun reached the outskirts of Sleepy Hollow. The Old Dutch Church lay ahead, its weathered stones bathed in pale moonlight. The surrounding cemetery was quiet, its headstones standing watch in the mist.

"This is it," Jackson said, pulling the Rover to a stop. "If the map's right, the next artifact is somewhere in the underground chambers."

Iris leaned forward in her seat, peering through the windshield at the familiar church. So much had happened since they'd first uncovered the clues that led them to this chase. Now, everything felt different. They were so close—too close to walk away.

Arjun, hunched over his laptop in the backseat, was typing furiously.

"I've scrambled any local surveillance systems," he

said. "We should be good for a while, but let's not linger."

Jackson turned off the engine, his expression tense.

"We get in, find the artifact, and get out. No unnecessary risks."

Iris nodded, but her mind was racing. The map she had taken from the lighthouse had led them there, and the compass Crane had given Jackson now pointed to a specific location deep beneath the church—somewhere they hadn't yet explored. She felt the magnitude of it all pressing on her. They weren't just looking for old artifacts anymore; they were in a race against people who wouldn't hesitate to kill for these pieces of the Seal.

"Let's go," Jackson said, reaching into the back to grab the bag with their tools and equipment. He handed Iris the compass, its needle faintly glowing as it pulsed in her hand. "You'll need this."

They stepped out into the night, their breath fogging in the chilly air. Arjun slung his bag over his shoulder, adjusting his glasses as he scanned the area. "If anyone's watching us, I can't detect them yet, but we're not exactly invisible."

They made their way through the cemetery and toward the hidden entrance to the underground chambers they had already discovered. The narrow stairs leading to the chambers beckoned, a cold draft rising from below. Iris flicked on her headlamp and led the way, the beam cutting through the darkness as they descended.

"Do you think the compass will work down here?"

Arjun asked, his voice echoing faintly in the cramped space.

Iris looked at the compass in her hand. "Crane wouldn't have given it to us if it couldn't lead the way."

They reached the bottom of the stairs, stepping into the underground chamber where they had once narrowly escaped an attack. The air was thick with the scent of damp earth and decay. Iris shivered but pressed forward, holding the compass in front of her. The needle spun wildly at first, then gradually steadied, pointing deeper into the maze-like tunnels.

"Looks like it's working," Jackson said, his voice low as he scanned their surroundings. "Crane told me to trust the compass."

The compass led them through a series of winding passages. Every step felt heavier as the sense of being watched crept over Iris. But it wasn't until they reached a narrow alcove that the compass began to pulse more rapidly, its needle pointing directly at a carved stone in the wall.

"This must be it," Iris said, her pulse quickening.

Jackson stepped forward, running his fingers over the stone. "There's a seam here. Here's hoping it's hollow behind this."

Arjun pulled a crowbar from his bag. "I've got this."

With a few careful movements, he pried the stone loose, revealing a small hidden compartment. Inside, resting on a velvet-lined base, was a metal object shaped like a star. It caught the faint light with a shimmer. Its surface was engraved with intricate patterns that matched the designs on the coin and compass they already had.

"The star." Iris exhaled, carefully lifting it from its resting place.

It felt warm to the touch, pulsing faintly, as if alive.

Jackson watched her closely.

"That's the third piece."

Arjun was already scanning the star with a device.

"It's definitely part of the Seal. But we need to figure out how it connects with the rest."

Iris tucked the star into her jacket pocket and zipped it, her heart pounding. "Let's get out of here first. We'll figure it out on the way to Crane's estate."

But before they could move, the sound of footsteps echoed down the hall behind them. Iris froze, her mind racing.

Jackson motioned for them to be quiet, stepping forward to peer down the tunnel.

"We've got company."

Iris whispered, "Make a run for it."

Without another word, they sprinted down the narrow passage, retracing their steps as the sound of footsteps grew louder behind them. Whoever was after them wasn't far.

They burst out of the underground chambers and into the cemetery, their breath coming in ragged gasps as they made for the car and piled in. Jackson floored the accelerator, and the car skidded out of the church-yard and onto the main road.

As they sped away, Iris clutched her chest, her heart

still racing. They had what they came for, but they were far from safe.

Jackson glanced at her, his jaw tight. "We've got the third piece. Now we just need the last one."

"The eagle," Iris said quietly.

Jackson nodded, his eyes focused on the road ahead.

THIRTEEN

The winding road narrowed as they drove deeper into the woods. The trees thickened, their gnarled branches casting shadows across the path, but Jackson kept sharp eyes on the road, navigating with practiced ease. The GPS blipped as they neared their destination, the old Crane estate.

"Up here," Jackson said quietly, gesturing toward a narrow offshoot from the main road. "We'll park just outside the grounds. The last thing we want is to get trapped inside."

Arjun nodded from the back seat, focused on his laptop.

"Good call. I've got a satellite map of the area. There's an old service road about a quarter mile from the estate's main gate. It's not on most modern maps, but it should give us a quick exit if things go south."

Iris glanced at Jackson. "Is it safe?"

"It's a road," Jackson replied, his jaw tight. "And our best shot at a quick getaway."

He turned off the main road, guiding the Land Rover down the gravel path that Arjun had marked. The road was overgrown, clearly unused for decades, but passable. Jackson steered the vehicle around overgrown brush and fallen branches, the headlights barely illuminating the dense thicket around them.

Finally, they reached a small clearing tucked behind a line of trees. Jackson pulled the car to a stop, shutting off the engine. The estate loomed just ahead, the towering spires of the Crane mansion barely visible through the thick foliage.

"This will do," Jackson said as he got out of the car. "We're close enough to move in on foot. But if anything goes wrong, there's enough cover to mask our route back."

Iris joined him, stepping out into the cool night air. The distant hoot of an owl and the rustling of the leaves reminded her of how isolated they were. She scanned the dark woods, noting how the dense trees provided cover but also made her uneasy.

Arjun picked up most of his gear but continued to work on his laptop.

"Let me run some final sweeps of the area for surveillance. We can't risk any surprises."

Jackson checked his watch, then looked up at the distant shape of the mansion. "We move in ten minutes."

Iris glanced at the map, feeling the weight of the eagle artifact in her pocket.

"Anyone else feel like this is too easy?" Arjun's voice came from the car. "I mean, we found the star. The map leads us right to the next piece. It's like... why aren't they here ahead of us?"

Iris glanced at Jackson, knowing Arjun had voiced the very fear that had been gnawing at her since they left the underground chambers.

"They're out there somewhere," Jackson said, his eyes focused on the road. "Maybe they think we haven't figured it out yet."

"Or they haven't figured it out, so they're waiting for us."

Iris didn't like it, but it had to be said.

Jackson sighed. "So, we do the hard work and find all the pieces."

A chill ran down Iris's spine. "And once we've done that..." She couldn't bring herself to finish the thought.

Jackson said, "That would explain why they haven't finished us off."

Iris shuddered. "Or we're simply a few steps ahead."

Jackson folded his arms. "We'll find out soon enough."

Arjun leaned out the window. "Hate to interrupt all your planning for our imminent demise, but some things can't be planned. But I've been monitoring what I could, and I've protected us with encryption, firewall,

VPN with a non-government cipher, antivirus of course, locked our SIM cards, and—"

"Arjun!" Jackson cut in. "Get to the point."

"We're still not invisible, so... If we're going to pull this off, we'll have to be quick."

Iris managed a faint smile at that. "Thanks, Arjun. We're ready when you are."

The road narrowed further as they approached Crane's estate, the woods giving way to the sight of an old iron gate looming ahead. It was rusted with age, covered in creeping ivy, and behind it stood the grand silhouette of the estate. The moonlight cast unsettling shadows across the sprawling mansion and grounds, which were overgrown with untamed grass and towering trees that swayed gently in the night breeze.

"Looks like something straight out of a Gothic novel," Iris muttered.

"Glowering Heights?" Arjun murmured.

Iris's heart thudded in her chest as they approached the gate—tall, sturdy, and locked. "Now what?"

Arjun looked up at the iron gate finials. "That's gotta hurt."

Iris walked past the gate and shone her flashlight on the imposing stone wall. "I don't know about you guys, but I think we're less likely to impale ourselves on this rock wall. Someone give me a hand?"

After struggling their way to the other side, Jackson said, "So much for getting in fast."

Iris refrained from pointing out that getting out wouldn't be any easier.

The gravel path crunched underfoot as they made their way toward the mansion, which loomed larger with every step. Dark windows stared down at them as if watching their approach.

As they neared the door, Jackson warned, "This place has been in Crane's family for generations. If the final piece is here, it won't be unguarded."

Iris took a deep breath and nodded.

They reached the front door, a massive, ornately carved wooden structure that looked as though it had stood for centuries. Jackson picked the lock and then pushed it open with a slow creak.

The interior was just as grand—yet unsettling—as the outside. A large foyer stretched before them, with a grand staircase spiraling upward into darkness. Paintings of long-dead ancestors lined the walls, their eyes seeming to follow the group as they entered.

"Not exactly minimalists, were they?" Arjun whispered, glancing around.

"Stay focused," Jackson said, pulling out the compass and holding it up. The needle swung wildly for a few seconds before settling on a direction, pointing them up the stairway.

"This way," Jackson said, leading the way as they followed the compass deeper into the mansion.

The air inside was cold and stale, as though no one had set foot here in years.

Iris felt a sense of unease growing with every step. Something about the mansion felt... wrong. The hairs on the back of her neck prickled.

"Does anyone else feel that?" she asked quietly.

"Yeah," Arjun replied with an uneasy waver. "Like we're not alone."

Jackson stopped at the end of the corridor, where the compass pointed to a door—a heavy wooden door, slightly ajar. "This is it."

Iris swallowed hard as they stepped inside. The room was a study, with old bookshelves lining the walls and a large, ornate desk in the center. But it was an object on the bookshelf that the compass led them to.

An intricately carved brass eagle sat on a shelf, its wings outstretched as if ready to take flight. It gleamed faintly in the room's low light as if it had been waiting for them.

"Is it just me, or does that seem a little too convenient?" Arjun asked, eyeing the eagle with suspicion.

Jackson approached it cautiously, reaching out to touch the artifact. The moment his fingers made contact with the eagle, the room seemed to shift. The air grew colder, and a low hum filled the room.

"Iris," Jackson called, his voice tense. "The star. Let's see if they fit."

Iris quickly pulled the star from her pocket. With steady hands, Jackson fitted the coin and the compass back-to-back and then placed the star into a matching notch on the coin side. He then turned it over, intently looking at Iris, and picked up the eagle. With a soft click, the last piece was in place. The eagle's wings fluttered as though coming to life.

A pulse of energy shot through the room, sending a

gust of wind swirling around them. Iris gasped as the energy rippled through her, like a current surging through her veins.

"This is it," he said, his voice low. "The final piece."

Arjun, who had been monitoring his phone, suddenly stiffened.

"Uh, guys... We've got a problem. The mansion's security system just kicked in, and I'm picking up movement outside."

Jackson cursed under his breath. "How long do we have?"

"Not long," Arjun said, glancing at the security feed on his phone. "They're closing in on us."

Iris's pulse quickened. "What do we do?"

Jackson turned to them, his expression calm but determined. "We find a way out or fight our way out."

With the final piece in hand, they had everything they needed—but now they had to survive long enough to use it.

FOURTEEN

The eerie quiet of Crane's estate was shattered by the pounding of footsteps and the low murmur of voices outside the building. Iris's heart raced as she exchanged a glance with Jackson, who tightened his grip on the eagle artifact they'd just retrieved. Arjun's face was pale, eyes glued to the laptop in front of him.

"They're closing in fast," Arjun muttered, his voice tight with fear. "We've got less than two minutes before they're right on top of us."

Jackson swore under his breath, then handed the eagle to Iris. "Keep this safe," he said firmly. She nodded, gripping the artifact tightly, though her hands trembled.

His eyes softened, though his tone remained resolute. "There's got to be a back stairway that leads out of this place."

Arjun's voice cracked as he spoke up. "Uh, not to

rain on your parade, but there's a lot of them. I count at least six... no, eight. Plus, they're packing serious heat."

Iris's chest tightened. Eight against the three of them? The odds didn't look good, but Jackson didn't falter. His expression remained unreadable as he quickly scanned their surroundings.

Arjun said, "According to the blueprints—"

Iris was stunned. "You've got blueprints?"

Arjun scrolled through his phone. "Well, yeah. To map out the security system. They're kind of hard to read on a phone screen." He headed for the door. Iris and Jackson exchanged looks, and then followed Arjun out of the library. "It should be over," he pulled open a door. "Here."

Jackson said, "Run," but Arjun was already halfway down the stairs, with Iris and Jackson close behind.

Arjun led them through corridors and connecting rooms running and, at times, stumbling through rooms lit only by slivers of moonlight that managed to find its way through gaps in the heavy draperies.

Arjun tapped and swiped at his phone as they moved, fingers flying. "I've rerouted their comms, but it won't last. They'll be confused for a few minutes—if we're lucky—but after that..." His voice trailed off, leaving the rest of the warning unsaid.

At last, hearing echoes of footsteps behind them, they reached a door leading out of the kitchen. A crash echoed through the estate, followed by the unmistakable sound of a gunshot.

"They're close," Arjun said, his voice barely above a whisper.

Jackson's eyes flicked toward the door. "Go," he said softly, pushing Iris and Arjun toward the narrow exit. "I'll hold them off."

"No!" Iris protested, panic rising in her throat. "With what? A skillet?"

"Just go," he said, his voice calm but firm. "We'll talk later."

Iris's heart screamed to stay, but her brain told her he was right. Without another word, she grabbed Arjun's arm and dragged him out the door and into the cold night air.

Behind them, the sound of gunfire erupted, a single shot ringing out in the dark. Iris's chest tightened in fear, every instinct telling her to run back, to make sure Jackson was okay. But there wasn't time. She couldn't stop. Not with the eagle in her possession.

They made it to the edge of the property, ducking behind a row of overgrown hedges. Arjun's hands trembled as he shoved his phone into his pocket, his eyes wide with fear.

"I didn't think it'd go this far," he whispered. "I thought we'd be in and out..."

"Shh," Iris hushed him, her own fear gnawing at the edge of her composure. She peered over the hedge, her heart pounding. "Just keep quiet and keep moving."

Another gunshot echoed from the estate, then another. A chill raced down Iris's spine, but she forced herself to focus. Jackson knew what he was doing. He'd outsmart them and get out. But how could he outsmart a gun?

Suddenly, the bushes in front of them rustled. Iris's heart leaped into her throat as a dark figure emerged from the shadows.

A man, one of the intruders, his gun raised.

Iris's pulse spiked. She acted on instinct, swinging the eagle artifact like a weapon, striking the man across the side of his head with a sharp crack. He collapsed to the ground, unconscious.

Arjun gaped. "Did you just—"

"Yes!" she hissed, dragging the unconscious man into the bushes before any of his companions could notice.

Before they could regroup, another figure appeared from behind the estate, heading their way. Iris glanced at Arjun. "We can't leave Jackson there, but if we stay here—"

Arjun's mind worked frantically. "If we could make it to the car, we could drive back for Jackson."

Iris nodded. "And do what? Pull up under the portico? Even if we had a meeting place, we'd be sitting ducks."

Arjun reluctantly nodded.

More footsteps approached. Iris braced herself, lifted the eagle and nearly struck Jackson. "Go," he commanded, his voice rough but intact. "They're not far behind."

They bolted for the woods, the cold night air biting at their skin. Behind them, the sounds of shouting and gunfire reverberated off the estate walls, but they didn't look back. They ran until their lungs burned, until the estate was nothing but a blur behind them.

They reached the edge of the forest, collapsing against the trunk of a towering tree, hearts pounding in their chests.

Jackson glanced down at the eagle, the artifact glinting in the moonlight. Between gasps of air, he said, "We need to finish what we started," he said, his voice steady. "And we're running out of time."

Jackson looked from Iris to Arjun, his face pale but determined. "Let's make a run for the car."

FIFTEEN

The Land Rover's engine hummed as they sped away from the Crane estate. Trees rushed past in a blur as Jackson drove down the shadowy road with sharp, focused intensity. Arjun sat in the back, typing furiously on his laptop, and Iris kept an eye on the rear window, scanning for signs of pursuers.

Her heart was still racing, the adrenaline from their narrow escape refusing to ebb. Her fingers curled tightly around the Seal, its cool surface grounding her in the chaos.

"Anyone following us?" Jackson's voice broke the tension, though his grip on the steering wheel was still taut, his jaw clenched.

Iris scanned the road behind them. "Nothing yet," she said, sounding surprisingly calm, though the knot of anxiety in her stomach wouldn't let go. "But now that they know we have the Seal, they won't stop."

Arjun didn't look up from his screen. "I'm diverting

any traceable signal we've left behind, but I can't guarantee it'll hold them off for long. Whoever's tracking us is good."

Jackson's eyes darted to the rearview mirror, his jaw set in a hard line. "We've got no choice. We can't let them catch up. Iris, just in case they do, disassemble the Seal, and divide the parts between us."

"Good idea. So, where are we headed?" Iris asked, gripping the eagle tighter.

Jackson's expression darkened. "I don't know. But we need to get there soon. The farther we go, the more exposed we are. They'll be watching the roads, trying to predict our next move."

Arjun spoke up from the back, his voice laced with urgency. "Guys, I just picked up a ping from one of the devices trying to locate us. They're back online. We can't outrun them forever if they've got this kind of tech."

"The tech," Jackson said, his voice calm but dangerous. "We've got to ditch it."

"Have you lost your mind?" Arjun asked, wide-eyed.

Iris's heart skipped a beat. "Jackson, Arjun's tech has saved us—more than once."

Jackson nodded, agreeing. "But it's also our Achilles' heel. As long as we can track them, they can track us."

Arjun hugged his laptop to his chest and shook his head slowly.

Keeping his eyes on the road, Jackson said, "Hear

me out. They'll find us no matter what. But if we go completely off-grid with no tech—full-out survivalist mode—we might stand a chance."

Iris eyed Jackson skeptically. "You want us to survive in the wild?"

He exhaled slowly. "I'm not talking forever. A few days—maybe a week."

Dismayed, Iris exhaled, her mind racing. "I'm not really very backwoodsy." She turned to Arjun, hoping for support, but he shook his head helplessly. And the look in Jackson's eyes told her they didn't have a choice. Their enemies weren't going to stop until they had the Seal.

Iris sighed, defeated. "Okay. I'll do it for the seal. But won't it be easier for them to detect us in the woods?"

Jackson said firmly. "We'll take measures to make sure that doesn't happen. Besides, we've got the Seal. If we can just figure out how to use it."

"That's a big 'if,'" Arjun muttered. "We don't have a clue what it's capable of."

Jackson's expression softened as he glanced at Iris. "Add that to our *to-do* list."

Iris swallowed hard, the eagle in her hands feeling heavier by the second. "So, where are we going?"

Jackson shifted in his seat, his eyes scanning the road ahead. "There's a state park up the road. It's large enough to get lost in, and at this time of year, end of season, it's practically empty."

"How far?" Arjun asked, his fingers still flying over the keys.

"I don't know... thirty minutes? Look up Fahnestock State Park." Jackson replied, his voice tense as he glanced in the rearview mirror again.

"Thirty-six minutes," Arjun corrected.

"If we're lucky, we'll have just enough time to camouflage the car, bury the tech, and head into the woods."

Iris nodded, trying to keep her fear at bay. "But state parks have park rangers."

Jackson said, "I didn't say the plan was perfect, but perfect isn't one of our options. I know of an old mining road, so, with luck, the park rangers won't know we're there. And if they tell us to leave, the Appalachian Trail runs through the park, so we could hike the trail."

Iris trusted Jackson's instincts, but this didn't seem like the most well-thought-out plan. "Wait. You just happen to know of an old mining road?"

Jackson shrugged. "It's a great place to hike, and there's a rail trail not far away."

For some reason, that surprised Iris. "You hike?"

"On occasion."

Iris added that to the lengthening list of things she didn't know about him. Another was how he proposed to survive.

After a quick stop at a convenience store to load up on provisions, they turned off the Taconic and onto a dirt path that wound through dense woods. The trees pressed in on either side, their branches casting long shadows like beckoning arms. The further they went, the rougher the terrain became, and the car bumped and jolted over the uneven ground.

Finally, after what felt like an eternity, Jackson pulled the Land Rover to a stop at the edge of a small clearing. The area was surrounded by thick trees and overgrown brush, the perfect cover for what they needed.

Jackson killed the engine and turned to face Iris and Arjun, his expression serious. "This is it."

Arjun winced as he erased all the tech, removed any SIM cards and batteries, placed it all in a trash bag, and buried it. Meanwhile, Iris and Jackson gathered branches and piles of leaves and camouflaged the SUV.

The moon was high in the sky by the time they finished, casting an eerie glow over the clearing. The forest was silent except for the occasional rustle of leaves in the wind.

Jackson stood at the edge of the clearing for a moment, his expression unreadable. Then he turned to Arjun and Iris. "Ready?"

Iris stood beside him, her heart pounding in her chest. She nodded, despite knowing she most absolutely was not.

"Here we go," Jackson said, his voice low.

Iris met his gaze and braced herself for what was to come.

FOR AN HOUR, they hiked through the woods in the dark and the cold.

Arjun quietly said, "You know, we have detectable heat signatures. All it will take is a helicopter to fly overhead with a thermal imaging device, and they'll find us."

Jackson didn't look surprised. "I picked up some mylar blankets when we stopped for supplies."

Arjun raised his eyebrows. "That'll work."

Iris knew she was frowning, but keeping silent was the best she could do. Her foot caught on a root, and she fell. As he helped her to her feet, Jackson drew her into his arms.

"Come here." As comforting as his embrace was, it wasn't enough to offset their dire situation.

Arjun gave Iris an encouraging look and then turned to Jackson. "We could all use a break."

With a nod, Jackson said, "You're right. We're no good exhausted."

They found a fallen log to sit on. Arjun pulled out a snack-sized bag of Doritos and offered it to the others. Iris thanked him but declined and pulled the old leather-bound journal from her bag, the one they'd grabbed in the tunnels. In all the excitement, they hadn't had a chance to examine it fully, and something about it was bothering her.

She flipped it open and pulled out a penlight. But when she caught a disapproving look from Jackson, she covered herself with a Mylar blanket to hide the light while she read. "There has to be something in here we're missing," she murmured, trailing her finger down the yellowed pages.

"Like what?" Arjun asked, while munching on chips.

Iris's eyes locked onto a passage she didn't remember seeing before.

WHERE RODE *a man on horse alight,*
  Across a bridge one hallowed night,
  Seek ye the place where Founders prayed,
  Though darker powers 'round you prey.

WHERE FREEDOM'S *flame once burned so bright,*
  Beneath the stars in shadowed night,
  Four parts assembled quell the fray,
  The Seal its power shall display.

"Guys?" She read the passage aloud, her voice barely a whisper at first, but as she repeated it, Arjun and Jackson both turned to look at her.

Jackson leaned closer, frowning. "Where the founders prayed... Church. The Old Dutch Church."

Iris nodded slowly. "It has to be. The church predates the Revolution. Washington and his men were known to have passed through the area."

Arjun's fingers stilled on his keyboard. "You think the final key to unlocking the Seal is... there?"

Iris shrugged. "I think that's what this says. I don't know. What I do know is that every lead seems to bring us back to Sleepy Hollow."

Jackson rubbed his chin. "So, the Old Dutch Church holds the key."

Arjun sat back, nodding slowly. "It's a place they wouldn't expect us to return to, that's for sure. And if there's something we missed, what better time to find it?"

Iris stared at the passage with a strange mix of relief and apprehension. "What else could it mean?"

Jackson stood, his face set with determination. "If it says to go there—and it seems to do just that—we should go."

"But first can we dig up the tech gear?"

SIXTEEN

The Old Dutch Church loomed ahead, its weathered stone façade almost glowing under the moonlight. It was late, and the churchyard was deserted. The towering oak trees swayed gently in the breeze, casting long, eerie shadows across the graves.

Iris, Jackson, and Arjun moved quickly and quietly toward the entrance, the book tucked under Iris's arm as she clung to the eagle.

"This is it," Jackson whispered, glancing around. "If the journal is right, the Seal's power will reveal itself here."

Arjun tapped on his phone, checking the feed from the traffic cams he'd hacked into. "No sign of them yet."

They slipped inside the darkened church, where the smell of old wood and stone filled the air. The silence was thick, as if the building itself held its breath.

Iris led them toward the front, where the founders

had once kneeled in prayer. She opened the book to the passage and read it again.

Where rode a man on horse alight,
Across a bridge one hallowed night,
Seek ye the place where Founders prayed,
Though darker powers 'round you prey.

WHERE FREEDOM'S flame once burned so bright,
Beneath the stars in shadowed night,

"THE STARS," Jackson muttered. "The windows."

He pointed toward the high arched window, where the starry night sky cast its light through the window. "The stars were thought to symbolize the heavens—divine guidance."

"Beneath the stars in darkest night..." Iris echoed, moving toward the pulpit. "It has to be here."

Suddenly, a flash of headlights illuminated the church's entrance. Iris's heart jumped into her throat. The Cassandra Collective had found them.

"We're out of time," Arjun hissed, his eyes darting to the doorway.

Jackson's eyes locked with Iris's, his resolve hardening. "Whatever this Seal does, it needs to do it now."

Arjun assembled the coin and the compass, and then Jackson inserted the star and set it on the stone altar. Iris held the eagle artifact in the light from the window. She took a deep breath and read the last lines of the rhyme once more.

Four parts assembled quell the fray,
The Seal its power shall display.

SHE INSERTED THE EAGLE, completing the Seal. The room seemed to hold its breath.

And then, as if in answer, the surrounding air shifted. A low hum vibrated through the church, growing in intensity as the Seal began to glow faintly. The light spread outward from the eagle, casting a shimmering, golden aura over the entire room.

The Seal had awakened.

The heavy wooden doors of the Old Dutch Church creaked open, and a voice echoed through the church.

Dr. Grice. The sound of his voice sent a chill through Iris. His presence was always unsettling, but tonight, the air around him felt malevolent.

He emerged from the shadows with Margaret Verplanck, the head of the Heritage Center, standing beside him, a look of sheer terror etched across her face. Her wrists were bound, and Grice pressed the barrel of a sleek pistol against her temple. "Doctors Drake and Wilde, here we are again, all together. I believe you know Margaret. She was working late, so I invited her to join us."

"Margaret!" Iris gasped, taking an involuntary step forward, but Jackson's hand shot out, stopping her. His eyes were locked on Grice, as if trying to read every movement.

Grice smiled, though it didn't reach his eyes. "Let's not waste time. I see you've come to appreciate the power of the Seal, although I doubt you fully understand it. We've been watching you."

"Who? Who's 'we'?" Iris's heart pounded as her grip on the eagle artifact tightened.

Grice's mouth spread into a half-smile. "But you know that already, don't you?"

"The Cassandra Collective," she answered.

Jackson's fingers brushed her arm, either as a silent reassurance or to caution her to be quiet. She wasn't sure which, but Jackson's tension was palpable.

"Very good. You've pieced together the clues, retrieved the artifacts, and you know it has power. But you don't know how to wield it. We, on the other hand, have known for centuries."

Grice continued, pacing leisurely in front of the altar. "The Cassandra Collective has been watching, biding our time. Your Founders may have created the Seal, but they did so out of fear—fear of change, fear of progress. The Collective knows better. Power isn't meant to be hidden away in dusty tomes or locked in relics. It's meant to be used."

"Used how?" Jackson's voice was low, tight. "To control people?"

Grice stopped pacing, turning his sharp gaze on Jackson. "Not control them—free them. This country has lost its way—corrupted by greed and materialism. The Seal has the power to course-correct, to transform the nation into what it should be."

"And what's that?" Iris shot back, her voice trembling with anger and fear. "This isn't about freeing anyone. It's about power for the sake of power."

"Your idealism is touching, Ms. Drake," Grice said with a smirk, "but misguided. People need a firm hand. Left to their own devices, they've squandered the ideals the Founders so naively entrusted them with. The Seal will allow us to rebuild, but better."

Margaret whimpered as the gun was pressed harder against her head. "Please," she whispered, her voice shaking. "Don't—"

Grice's voice was too low to hear, but whatever he said in her ear silenced her.

Iris's chest tightened. They couldn't let Margaret die. But how could they release the Seal into the hands of someone like Grice?

Jackson's voice was steady but laced with fury. "You think killing innocent people will bring order?"

Grice tilted his head, the smug smile never leaving his face. "For the greater good. A nation's people are like a family. We all have a role. For some, that role is sacrifice."

Arjun, who was surrounded by the tech gear he hadn't set up, muttered under his breath, "And I thought my family reunions were bad."

Jackson's hand touched hers, no doubt meant to

reassure her, but she could feel the tension rolling off him. Time was running out.

"We don't have a choice," Jackson whispered, his voice tinged with regret. "We can't let them kill her."

Iris's heart sank. She knew he was right. They were different from Grice. Even one life was too great a sacrifice. They couldn't sacrifice Margaret, but handing over the Seal felt like a death sentence of a different kind.

Iris's hand trembled as she put her hand on the Seal. Glowing energy hummed through it, resonating throughout the church. Her heart hammered as she lifted it.

"Wise decision." Grice's eyes gleamed with triumph as he handed off Margaret to one of his henchmen and stepped forward.

Iris hesitated, her eyes meeting Jackson's. His jaw was clenched, the regret clear in his gaze. Slowly, she handed over the Seal.

The instant Grice's fingers closed around it, the atmosphere in the church changed. The air seemed to crackle with energy as the Seal's glow grew brighter in Grice's hands.

And then something unexpected happened.

The guns—every single one held by Grice and the Collective—began to glow with the same eerie light as the Seal. The men exchanged nervous glances, but before anyone could react, the metal began to heat up. The barrels sizzled and hissed, turning white hot.

One by one, the Collective members cried out in pain, dropping their weapons as they became too hot to handle. The guns clattered to the stone floor, smoking and warping as they started to melt, dissolving into molten metal, and vaporizing into thin air.

"What is this?" Grice's voice was sharp, his calm demeanor crumbling as the Seal's power surged out of his control. "What have you done?"

Iris stood frozen, her eyes wide. "We didn't do anything..."

The Seal glowed brighter, its light filling the church. The Collective members panicked. With their hands burned and their confidence shattered, they turned and fled through the church doors, abandoning their leader.

Dr. Grice, teeth clenched in fury, pointed an accusing finger at Iris and Jackson. "This isn't over," he snarled. "You will live to regret this!" With that, he flew out of the door and disappeared into the night.

As the doors swung shut behind him, Margaret stumbled forward, her knees buckling as she collapsed onto a pew, gasping for breath. Jackson was at her side in seconds, his arm around her shoulders, steadying her.

Iris's heart pounded in her chest, still absorbing what had just happened. The Seal had done something —something beyond their understanding, something powerful. It had protected them—and whoever the Collective might have harmed, perhaps even the nation.

Arjun's voice cut through the tension in the air. "Well," he said, glancing around at his melted firearms, "I guess we can cancel that order for bulletproof vests."

Iris couldn't help but laugh, a burst of relief

washing over her as she went to give Arjun a hug. The tension broke, and even Jackson cracked a weary smile as he helped Margaret to her feet.

For a brief moment, in the quiet aftermath of the storm, they stood together in the pale moonlit church, the Seal's glow fading into a gentle, warm pulse. They had survived.

SEVENTEEN

Weeks had passed since that night at the Old Dutch Church, but the memory of it lingered in the air. The town had returned to its sleepy, peaceful self, and the church now stood as a quiet symbol of something far greater than its weathered stones suggested.

Iris stood outside the church, her gaze drifting over the graveyard, where sunlight now warmed the head-stones. The Seal was safe, hidden once more, its true power understood only by a select few.

Jackson stepped up beside her and slipped his hand into hers. "We did it," he said softly, his voice carrying a mix of relief and quiet wonder.

She smiled, glancing at him. "We did."

There was so much more to do—so many questions were left unanswered about the Seal and its future. But for now, they had peace.

And in that moment, standing beneath the stars

that had once guided the founders, Iris felt as though history had settled back into place. In the back of her mind, she knew there would always be more to do—more to protect, more to uncover, more to fight for.

But at this moment, she was content to stand here with Jackson, both knowing they'd faced something far bigger than themselves—and come out the other side.

THANK YOU!

Thank you for reading! If you enjoyed this book, please consider leaving a review or a rating on Amazon or your favorite bookstore. Your feedback helps other readers discover my work.

READ THE EXCITING CONCLUSION
IN BOOK 3 OF THE DRAKE &
WILDE MYSTERIES

In Sleepy Hollow, history doesn't rest... and neither do its secrets.

When historian Iris Drake takes a job as a tour guide in Sleepy Hollow, she expects to share tales of headless horsemen and haunted bridges. Instead, a chance encounter with the enigmatic and brilliant Professor Jackson Wilde plunges her into a centuries-old conspiracy that could rewrite American history.

As Iris and Jackson race to decode cryptic messages left by the Founding Fathers, they uncover a world of hidden chambers, shadowy societies, and a mysterious "covenant" guarded by the Wardens of Liberty. With each clue bringing them closer to the truth—and to each other—the line between ally and enemy blurs.

Their growing attraction only heightens the stakes

as they find themselves pursued by those who would keep the past buried. In a town where legend and reality intertwine, Iris must decide how much she's willing to risk for the truth... and for love.

Because in Sleepy Hollow, some secrets are worth killing for – and others might just save a nation. But in a town where nothing is as it seems, who can they trust? Dive into the mystery today!

Find out more at
jljarvis.com/shadow/

BOOK NEWS

Sign up for the J.L. Jarvis Journal for exclusive benefits, including free books, special offers, exclusive content, and updates on new releases: news.jljarvis.com

READING ORDER

Drake & Wilde Mysteries

#1 *Love in the Time of Pumpkins*

#2 *Secrets in the Hollow*

#3 *Shadow of the Horseman*

Standalones

A Kiss in the Rain

App-ily Ever After

Once Upon a Winter

The Red Rose

Highland Vow

Short Stories

Seasons of Love: A Short Story Collection

The Eleventh-Hour Pact

A Christmas Yarn

The Farmer and the Belle

Work-Crush Balance

Cedar Creek

(Can be read in any order)

Christmas at Cedar Creek

Snowstorm at Cedar Creek

Sunlight on Cedar Creek

Pine Harbor

(Reading Order)

#1 *Allison's Pine Harbor Summer*

#2 *Evelyn's Pine Harbor Autumn*

#3 *Lydia's Pine Harbor Christmas*

Holiday House

(Can be read in any order)

The Christmas Cabin

The Winter Lodge

The Lighthouse

The Christmas Castle

The Beach House

The Christmas Tree Inn

The Holiday Hideaway

Highland Passage

(Can be read in any order)

Highland Passage

Knight Errant

Lost Bride

Highland Soldiers

(Reading Order)

#1 *The Enemy*

#2 The Betrayal

#3 The Return

#4 The Wanderer

American Hearts

(Can be read in any order)

Secret Hearts

Forbidden Hearts

Runaway Hearts

For more information, visit jljarvis.com.

Get monthly book news at news.jljarvis.com.

ABOUT THE AUTHOR

J.L. Jarvis is a left-handed former opera singer/teacher/lawyer who writes books. She now lives and writes on a mountaintop in upstate New York.

jljarvis.com

f facebook.com/jljarvis1writer

X x.com/JLJarvis_writer

instagram.com/jljarvis.writer

BB bookbub.com/authors/j-l-jarvis

pinterest.com/jljarviswriter

g goodreads.com/5106618.J_L_Jarvis

a amazon.com/author/B005G0M2Z0

youtube.com/UC7kodjlaG-VcSZWhuYUUl_Q

www.ingramcontent.com/pod-product-compliance
Lightning Source LLC
Chambersburg PA
CBHW020907180626
46816CB00007BA/2288